Blind Spot
CHRIS FABRY

TYNDALE HOUSE PUBLISHERS, INC., CAROL STREAM, ILLINOIS

Blind Spot

CHRIS FABRY

RPM

RPM
1

Library of Congress Cataloging-in-Publication Data

Fabry, Chris, date.
  Blind spot / Chris Fabry.
    p. cm. — (RPM ; #1)
  Summary: For Tim Carhardt and Jamie Maxwell, life has been all about NASCAR racing, but while Tim's only goal is to survive, Jamie is determined to become the first successful female driver, and both find themselves tested when dreams and faith collide.
  ISBN-13: 978-1-4143-1264-4 (softcover)
  ISBN-10: 1-4143-1264-4 (softcover)
[1. Automobile racing—Fiction. 2. Sex role—Fiction. 3. Christian life—Fiction. 4. Stock car racing—Fiction. 5. NASCAR (Association)—Fiction.] I. Title.
  PZ7.F1178Bli 2007
  [Fic]—dc22   2007006084

Printed in the United States of America

13	12	11	10	09	08	07
7	6	5	4	3	2	1

This book is dedicated to Jan and Brian, who had the idea.

> **"No man is truly ready to live until he is no longer afraid to die."**

Adrian Rogers

> **"Talladega is one of those places that will make you religious pretty quick."**

Ryan Pemberton, Crew Chief—#01 Army Chevrolet
From A Week in the Life of NASCAR: A View from Within

Blind spot:

A part of an area that cannot be directly observed.

CONTEXT IS EVERYTHING. A wonderful story about sports becomes even more meaningful when you understand what's gone on behind the scenes. A young rookie's first game makes a good story, but when it's Jackie Robinson breaking the color barrier of the all-white Major League Baseball, it becomes historic. College all-stars banding together to form a hockey team is exciting, but when that team wins an Olympic gold medal in 1980, it's a dream come true.

These stories would command our attention even if we didn't know what went on in the lives of the participants. But when you understand more about the people, their struggles, the overwhelming obstacles they faced in their personal lives, then they become unforgettable.

Foreword

That's why I'm so excited about the RPM series. Rarely do you get to see the authentic beginnings of something so special. So pure. I've covered NASCAR a lot of years. I remember what happened that year like it was yesterday—how Jamie made a mark on the sport at such a young age and the tragedy that hit Tim. As an insider who loves to write about the sport and watch the action on the track, I think this is a one-of-a-kind memoir.

I wish I'd written this story, but I wasn't on the inside. I wish I'd lived half of the adventure, but I didn't. I wish I'd somehow seen what would happen before the curtain ever lifted on the lives of the people of Velocity, North Carolina. But who am I kidding? The story is right here for you. Every bit of it. And the best part is, there's nothing left out.

Read and enjoy their tale. And while you're at it, go and make some history of your own someday.

Calvin Shoverton

Motorsports Senior Reporter, Charlotte Times

THAT OCTOBER SUNDAY afternoon in Talladega, Alabama, changed Tim Carhardt's life forever. After applying the weather-strip adhesive to the lug nuts, securing and covering them, he had moved to the grandstands.

"Too many people in the pits makes a bad day," his dad had said with the kind of frown that told Tim there was nothing his dad could do. People on the team were edgy. The owner paced from the pit area to the garage, as nervous as a slow mouse in a room full of fast cats.

Instead of chowing down on the food Tim's dad had cooked for the team, the crew picked at it with blank stares and none of the normal wisecracks or practical jokes. Everybody could sense something in the air. Whether it was good or bad, Tim couldn't tell, but you could cut the tension with a butter knife.

Maybe it was the fact that the driver, Kenny Overton, had announced his retirement two weeks earlier, and everybody was wondering if another team would pick them up next year. Tim's dad had already found work. It was just a matter of finishing the season and heading north. A good driver who could cook *and* lift a heavy gas can was valuable.

Tim grabbed his dad's beat-up binoculars from the hauler and slipped the grandstand pass around his neck. He liked watching from the pits and helping his dad do the gas runs, but the stands would be okay. At least the crew chief didn't make him sit in the hauler through the race. He'd had that happen a time or two when he was younger.

He passed concessions, and his mouth watered at the smells of bratwurst and onions. Nothing better than a huge corn dog slathered with mustard. Or a cherry limeade to wash it down. But he had only a couple of dollars in his pocket. Maybe if Overton won today, his dad would give him the traveling cash he'd promised, but Tim wasn't holding his breath. Money was always tight.

Tim scanned the stands. The faces were a blur in the sunshine. Women with skimpy outfits, sunglasses, and big hair. Men yelling for their favorite drivers as motorcycles, flags, and celebrities passed by in the parade.

These people had no idea what it was really like to put cars on the track. They got to go home after the race and watch reruns on SPEED and maybe catch a football game. Put their feet up and eat pizza and enjoy their big-screen TV. Tim spent the hours after a race packing up and running around. After the all-day race preparations, bone tired and hungry, he'd spend the night trying to get comfortable in the passenger side of Charlie Hale's 18-wheeler, with the split in the seat and a beagle—Chester—that smelled like the south end of a northbound cow. Actually, he smelled more like a donkey. They'd drive all night to North Carolina and then unload and make preparations for the next race.

But Tim wouldn't trade being this close to the action, where people in the stands could only dream of being. Early one morning, as he was helping his dad set up for breakfast, two drivers in the top 10 in points had been talking about conditions at the track as Tim walked by with bags of ice for the cooler. One of the drivers asked Tim for a couple of sodas. Tim knew which ones to bring because these guys wouldn't be caught dead drinking anything but their sponsor's soda. The logos were all over their fire suits and the quarter panels of their cars. One driver gave him $20 when he came back with the sodas. That was the kind of thing that could happen if you were in the right place at the right time.

But Tim wanted to do more than just fetch Coca-Cola. He wanted to drive. He dreamed of seeing himself in one of those suits someday, racing around the track, taking the checkered flag, shaking a bottle of champagne until it fizzed all over everybody. If that ever happened, the first people he would thank would be the guys who did all the grunt work. Guys like his dad. They never complained. Just did their jobs and made things comfy for everybody else.

The closest Tim had ever gotten to racing was riding go-karts at an amusement park. But he was sure if he ever got the chance, he could show people he was something special.

The people in the stands wore the numbers of their favorite drivers and cheered when they were introduced and walked across the makeshift stage, but they had no idea how important the team was. The crew. Without them, the driver was nothing. Of course, without the driver, the crew was nothing too. Tim felt like the fans talked about teamwork and gave credit to the crew chief or the spotter, but they didn't really know that everyone wearing the uniform had to work together like pistons in an engine. And everything had to fire just right, at the exact moment, in order to win.

Drivers and crew members lined up for the prayer and the national anthem. Then it was some

guy from Hollywood or Nashville or New York saying, "Gentlemen, start your engines!" He was probably another celebrity whose first trip to the track was
today.

Switches flipped and engines roared. The track
came to life. Tim turned on his scanner and locked
in to the right channel. With his headphones in place,
he could hear every word the spotter and crew chief
said to the driver.

"Come on," he whispered, focusing on Overton's
#12 car. "This is it. This is the big one."

The crowd yelled as the cars picked up speed, the
pace car veered off, and the green flag waved. The
engines whined like a million screaming fans, and
it overwhelmed him as always. It made him feel like
he was caught up in something bigger than himself.
Something huge and unbelievably earsplitting.

Tim was high in the stands, focused on #12 as the
car hit the back straightaway. Already the cars had to
be going somewhere between 190 and 200 mph.

Fans yelled their favorite drivers' names as the
train of cars roared by. *Ffft, ffft, ffft, ffft.* Hats flew off
at the railing seconds later.

"Outside, at your shoulder," the spotter said. "At
your door. Clear. Clear."

Tim looked at the stands again. The crowd moved
like a living thing, an undulating ocean of people. It

was a multicolored sea of hats and shirts with every number of every driver from 30 years ago to the present. Some were faded. Some were right off the rack from the vendors outside. A face caught his eye. A woman moved in the stands, crossing a few rows in front of him, staring. Hat pulled low. Sunglasses. Red and black T-shirt. Brown hair flowing from under her hat and down her back.

Tim stood, his binoculars dropping to his chest. Was it the same shirt he'd seen in the pictures?

The woman disappeared into the tunnel below.

He wiped sweat from his brow. Should he follow her? She looked so much like her. Maybe it *was* her. But what would she be doing here? He shook it off as a coincidence, but the eerie feeling stayed.

Finally Tim couldn't stand it any longer, and he ran down the stairs and into the tunnel. It was a little cooler here. The smell of food was overpowering.

Women were lined up near the bathrooms and stood shifting from one foot to the other. Talking. Laughing. A few of them headed out to the green Porta Potties. Several men straggled out of the bathroom, hurrying back to their seats, getting their earplugs in place.

Tim looked both ways at streams of people. Hundreds of them. Some were latecomers. Others were just hot-dog hounds or beer guzzlers. He couldn't shake the sight of the woman, and he started weaving in and out of the crowd. He neared another women's restroom and saw brown hair.

"Hey, watch it!" a burly guy shouted as Tim bumped him. He balanced two drinks and a mustard-covered pretzel.

"Sorry," Tim said, still moving.

He ran as the woman turned the corner and ascended the steps. A roar from the crowd. Something was happening.

The woman stopped at the top by a security guard. She clapped and hopped, her hat falling to the ground as a gust of wind caught it.

Tim picked it up and handed it to her. His heart fluttered as she turned and looked him full in the face.

"Thanks, young man." The woman was a lot older than his mother, with bronze skin—like a lizard's. She wore enough lipstick to paint Interstate 20 all the way to Atlanta. Her eyes crinkled, and she drawled, "Is there something wrong, sweetheart?"

Tim looked down. "No. I thought you were somebody else. Sorry."

A hollow feeling dogged him as he hiked back to his seat. He checked the lap count and the leader. They were 25 laps into the race, and so far there hadn't been a crash. Talladega was the longest track for cup races, the scene of horrendous crashes. The fans around him seemed antsy, anticipating the big one, the worst crash of the day.

On the back turn a car spun out, sending a plume of white smoke in the air. The yellow flag came out.

"Crash in turn three. Back it down," the spotter said. "I don't see many pieces out there—just follow the car in front of you."

Tim looked at the Overton pit crew as they sprang to life. Another lap behind the pace car and the race for the pits would be on.

Tim found his dad in the flurry of activity among the red suits. They were the second stall coming off the track—a difficult position. The fireman was just behind the wall with an extinguisher nearby. The race officials were there too, ready to eye the stop.

Tim clicked the black button on his watch until he came to the 00:00 on his stopwatch. Car #12 veered onto pit road and screeched to a halt, three tires inside the box.

"That counts," Tim whispered, watching the official. "Come on, guys."

The crew was over the wall before the car stopped, and Tim pushed the button. Precious seconds ticked by as Tim's father moved into position. He was the catch can man.

:03

The rear tires were off. They were having a good stop. The jackman let the car down and raced around the front, carrying the jack as if it weighed nothing, which Tim knew wasn't true. He had lifted the thing with one hand—or at least tried to.

:09

They might have him out in :13, a serious pit stop!

The crowd gasped and Tim looked up, away from the binoculars. Another car barreling toward pit road had lost control, its back end swerving. It was coming too fast to stop, too fast to gain control. Then came a sickening crunch and people scurrying. Smoke and debris.

Tim's heart beat wildly as he stood, straining to see what had happened. An ambulance parked at the other end of the track pulled out and made the long trip around.

"Did somebody get hit?" Tim said to a guy beside him.

"I didn't see it," the man said. "My wife said she thought there was somebody caught between the two cars."

He ran up the grandstand and sprinted for the path that led him to the infield. He knew he couldn't get back inside, but he had to do something. His headset crackled, and he heard the spotter cutting in and out, saying #12 was out of the race and so was the other car, #14. Were the drivers hurt? someone on the crew?

The ambulance raced toward the track hospital as Tim reached the security guards.

"Timmy!" someone called. It was Charlie Hale, another member of the Overton crew, his face ashen, eyes red. "You can't go back there, son."

"Who was it?" Tim said. "I saw that car come flying in there out of control."

"You haven't heard?" Charlie's chin puckered and he looked away. "It was a mess all right."

When the man shoved his hands into his back pockets, Tim knew. "How bad is he?"

"Aw, Timmy," was all Charlie could say. He put an arm around Tim and pulled him close. "I'm real sorry."

"He's at the hospital, right? I mean, they'll be able to help him there."

Charlie didn't answer.

The rotors turned on the medevac helicopter. Two men with security badges came toward them. "Are you Tim Carhardt?" one of them said.

The men stood on either side of him, holding him up as if he was going to collapse. A police car was waiting for him in the parking lot, its lights flashing. The chopper took off, and Tim got in the cruiser.

As they pulled away, a rumble of engines sounded as the green flag came out. The race was under way again.

THE SNOW BOLL IS HELD mid-January each year near Enterprise, Alabama. The title comes from a statue in the middle of the town—a white-gowned lady holds a black bug over her head, and a fountain around her sprays water. The bug is a boll weevil, and the town pays tribute to the pesky critter that destroyed cotton crops in the early 1900s. The boll weevil forced farmers to turn to other crops, like peanuts. At the bottom of the statue is a plaque that reads, "In profound appreciation of the Boll Weevil and what it has done as the Herald of Prosperity."

Every year an ice sculpture of a boll weevil is made, and a snow machine sprays slush on the grandstands at the "Coffee County Speedway," a three-quarter-mile racetrack. Young and old travel to the race on foot and tractors, and there's even a school bus competition. But the premier event is the Saturday night Legends race called the Snow Boll. Cars from 25 states qualify in the afternoon, and the excitement builds to a crescendo as the sun goes down.

Everyone's favorite driver is a local 63-year-old furniture salesman who does TV commercials in his racing suit and helmet, sitting on one of his patented "comfortable recliners." However most of the entrants are younger.

This year the pole-position and second-place drivers were kids of current NASCAR drivers Butch Devalon and Dale Maxwell, and it was clear that the rivalry of the fathers had been visited on their offspring.

After the National Anthem, sung by the First Baptist Church choir, the cars revved their engines, and the race began. Some of the drivers, like the furniture salesman, were content to stay in the back of the pack, but it was obvious from the moment the green flag waved that there were two who were serious about winning the Boll.

Car #13, Chad Devalon, zoomed around the track, a good four car lengths ahead of #76, Jamie Maxwell. The two had led every lap of the race.

A man in black jeans with a black jacket and #13 on both shoulders hooted, "You got it, Chad! Pour it on, buddy!"

A female fan approached with a folded T-shirt and a Sharpie.

"Not now, darlin'; I'm watchin' my son," the man said. Then he yelled, "Take it to 'em, Chad!"

Each time he yelled, the people around him inched away. The tension seemed to float through this roped-off section like bad exhaust through a garage. He pumped a fist in the air and rattled the chain-link fence with the other hand.

Several rows away, studying the race like a hawk watches a field for movement, a woman with long red hair focused on #76. Anyone who knew racing could tell she was studying the line of the car as it settled into the black groove of the track—the best path for the fastest speed. As the car rounded the far turn, the woman's body swayed, as if a part of her were in the car. "Come on, Jamie," she whispered through clenched teeth.

Beside the woman was a small boy with darker skin than hers, brown eyes as big as saucers, and a NASCAR hat pulled low. He rolled his eyes and frowned as Butch Devalon yelled again. The boy looked up at the man next to him, who was scrolling through messages on a cell phone. "Which is worse, Dad? Driving against him or sitting near him during a race?"

The man smiled. He had an understated *MM* on his hat and a tanned, weathered face. "Not sure. Both are pretty frustrating."

"Punch it, Chad!" Butch Devalon hollered. "Take it!"

The nearest car to the two leaders was #88, driven by a local kid who barely fit into the car. His helmet looked tight, pushing his cheeks out like a chipmunk's with a full winter's worth of stored nuts.

The announcer's voice blared over the loud-speaker. "Ten laps to go and Chad Devalon has a slim lead over Jamie Maxwell."

Cheers went up around the stands as the names were called. These two were only in high school, and they already had a following.

The announcer ran through the rest of the field, with the furniture salesman getting the biggest applause.

"Here comes Jamie," Kellen said to his dad.

Jamie's dad looked up from his phone to the first turn, where #76 moved to the inside and shot past #13. He smiled and whistled as the crowd responded.

"Come on, Chad!" Butch Devalon shouted. "Show us what you can do!"

The smells of engine oil, gasoline, and exhaust hung in the air, mixed with corn dog batter and chicken. The moon rose over the horizon like a white face looking down on the race from the best seat in the sky.

The #76 driver wore a yellow fire suit a couple

of sizes too big and an orange helmet marked and scarred from use, as if both were hand-me-downs. In car #13, the driver wore a black helmet that reflected the track lights like a shiny mirror.

With six laps to go, the #13 car bumped the leader in turn two, but #76 gained control and, it seemed, more speed and shot into the straightaway confident.

Butch Devalon cursed and didn't seem to notice the angry stares around him.

"Jamie's gonna do it, Dad!" Kellen said.

Jamie's mom bounced on her seat, balling her fists and smacking the fence just in front of her. "Come on, Jamie!"

The two cars ran inches apart, screaming around the turns, and the crowd roared. The white flag came out as they approached the start/finish line.

People stood and moved closer to the fence, grabbing on, straining to see, whooping and yelling and pumping their fists.

"Looks like he's gaining ground," Jamie's dad muttered to Kellen.

Butch Devalon shook the fence and yelled, "You got it! Now take it, Chad!"

The cars ran like mirror images around the first two turns. In the backstretch, #13 went low and tried to pull even, but #76 followed down, blocking the move. Into turn three, #76 followed the groove perfectly, accelerating into turn four and shooting out like a bullet.

It looked like #76 had a lock on the finish line until #13 also shot forward and low, barely pulling up enough to reach the back end of #76, then swerving right, clipping the back of #76 and sending the car into a slow spin. White smoke rose from the tires, and #13 swerved left and crossed the finish line as the checkered flag flew.

The #76 car spun completely around and veered onto the infield, creating brown marks in the grass. When it came to a stop, the driver slammed the steering wheel with both fists and spun the tires.

The crowd groaned, stunned by the move, but Butch Devalon pumped his fist in the air and cheered. He looked down at Jamie's family and flashed his patented smirk as #13 took a victory lap, then spun in the infield grass near where #76 had stopped.

"That's dirty racing," someone said behind Jamie's mom.

"Just like his daddy," another said.

"Uh-oh," a man said, pointing. "Looks like there's gonna be a fight!"

The #76 driver had almost climbed out of the car and was pointing at the #13 driver. Chad Devalon just waved at the crowd, half of them booing him, and took off his black helmet. When he saw the other driver coming, he put the helmet under his arm and gave a smirk frighteningly similar to the one his dad had given the family.

"What'd you say?" Chad said, one arm out, as innocent as a baby. He was taller than the approaching driver but not by much.

The orange helmet came off and a ponytail fell. "You did that on purpose and you know it!" Jamie Maxwell yelled.

"Hey, it's just one of those racing things," Chad said, moving back toward his car. "If you can't take the heat, don't get on the track."

"I *can* stand the heat. I can't stand a *cheat*."

Chad shook his head. "Face it, Maxwell. You're just like your old man. You don't have what it takes to be out here."

By now the section for fans had opened, and people poured onto the track, led by Butch Devalon. "Better get her away from my son, Maxwell. Hate to see that pretty little girl of yours get a black eye."

"You should teach your son not to drive dirty!" the boy yelled back.

"Kellen, that's enough," Jamie's mother said. She called her daughter over to them.

Jamie was near tears, but she steeled her face and fought them back. "I can't believe he did that."

Jamie's dad patted her shoulder and walked with her, inspecting the damage to the car. "You gotta learn to just walk away. You can't waste your rep on a guy like that."

"Hey, Maxwell," Butch Devalon called. He was signing T-shirts and leaning against his son's car. "You should have her stop driving and start babysitting. You could use the sponsorship."

"See what I mean?" Jamie said. "It's hard not responding to that."

Jamie's father wiped his forehead and knelt on the ground by the car's mangled rear end. He nodded to the fans streaming onto the infield. "You see all those people? You never know when one of them will turn out to be a scout. And one slipup, one time that you let your emotions get the best of you, and you can bet somebody'll get it on video, and then it's all over."

"His reputation doesn't seem to be bothering him," Jamie said, nodding toward Butch Devalon.

"It's gonna catch up with him one of these days," Jamie's dad said. Several girls were running toward Jamie's car. "Now shake it off and go say hi to your fans."

Jamie took a deep breath and blew it out.

The girls held out scraps of paper, and one of them said, "I just know we're gonna see you racing someday in NASCAR."

"I hope so," Jamie said.

Butch Devalon walked by and the girls swooned, pushing their paper in his direction. He ignored them and looked right at Jamie. "Not half bad for a girl," he said. "Now you gotta learn how to finish." He faced Jamie's dad. "But you'll have to get a new teacher if you want to do that."

Jamie wanted to turn back and tell him off, but she couldn't think of anything to say. Tomorrow she would. Some snappy comeback that would put the guy in his place. But nothing came now. She was too mad about what had been taken away.

JAMIE MAXWELL STARED out the window of the Chevy Suburban. She couldn't stand to look at the car they towed, its back end mangled. She could probably get it fixed before the next race, but she couldn't get this one out of her mind.

Her mom had only opened her mouth when Jamie shot back, "I don't want to talk about it."

"It was all I could do to keep from decking that guy," Kellen said. "I could have beat him up, you know."

Jamie smiled. Her little brother sticking up for her always made her smile. He was a major pain most of the time, annoying the rest. But he had a cute way of getting under her skin. She pictured him standing on tiptoes, reaching up to hit Chad.

A driving January rain fell sideways

through the beam of the headlights. They had planned on staying the night just outside Montgomery, but with all the tension in the car, no one felt like sleeping, so they decided to drive the eight hours home.

The headlights flashed on the rippling surface of a lake by the road. *Perfect weather for the way I feel.*

"That's exactly what Chad wanted," her dad said over the swish-swish of the windshield wipers.

"What do you mean?" Kellen said.

Her dad looked over at her mom, who shifted in her seat, stretching her arms and yawning.

"Kids like Chad are taught to win at any cost," her mom said. "When they can't win, they just try to tear down the competition. Any way they can."

"Like that election you were talking about, Dad?" Kellen said.

"What?" Jamie said, scrunching her face and giving Kellen a look. "What's an election got to do with—?"

"Dad said the guy running for senator a few months ago didn't have any ideas. He just tried to . . . say bad things about his opponent so people would vote for him. It's kinda like that, isn't it?"

"Only Chad didn't just use words," her dad said. "He could have really hurt somebody."

"Then why don't they do something about it?" Jamie muttered. "It's not like this is the first time."

Her mom sighed as their tires splashed in pot-holes. "Chad has talent. He's a good driver with quick reflexes and a fearless attitude. But he knows you're better. And if he can get you mad and make you start throwing punches—" she glanced at Jamie—"which I know you would *never* do, he can take you out without having to beat you on the track."

"Can't drive NASCAR with a temper," Kellen said. "That's what you say all the time, isn't it, Dad?"

"You got that right," her dad said. "You have to keep your head, control your anger—"

"Can we talk about something else?" Jamie said. "Like those meetings you two are always going to?"

Her dad gave her mom a look and reached forward. "Let's just listen to the radio."

A soft country song played—something about dreams dying and a love lost. The biggest problem Jamie had with Chad Devalon was not that he was mean on the track but that she felt something for him inside—and she hated herself for it. Why couldn't she get interested in some of the guys at her youth group? Why did she have feelings for such a jerk?

Because he was cute. That had a lot to do with it.

The only time she forgot about her troubles was when she was on the track. There, with the helmet on and the shield down and the buzz of the engine behind her, she was locked in another world. When she was there, the meanest teacher, the worst prima donna at school, and all the teasing by the other kids about being a girl in a guy's world couldn't touch her.

Jamie could understand why her dad spent so much time at the garage and in preparation for the season. It was her dream too. Her goal was to be the first female cup winner in history.

She put her head against the window and let the sound of the road lull her to sleep.

When Jamie woke up, lightning flashed in the distance, illuminating the green sign that said "Velocity, NC. Population 6,495." They pulled up the gravel drive and parked in the open barn, out of the weather.

"We'll unload later," her dad said. "Everybody get inside and get some sleep."

Kellen hopped out first and stumbled toward the house.

The barn still had the smell of hay in it, but there hadn't been a horse or cow here since the Maxwells had bought the place.

"Jamie, how would you feel about watching your brother tomorrow night?" her mother said, yawning.

Jamie rolled her eyes. "Where're you going this time?"

"It's our last class."

"What class? What are you guys doing?"

Her mom smiled and cocked her head at Jamie, the falling rain behind her, her face silhouetted in the overhead light.

"Oh, all right," Jamie said. "But I want combat pay."

THE TRAILER PARK SAT NEAR the Apalachicola National Forest, about 30 miles from the Gulf of Mexico, but to Tim Carhardt, the gulf felt as far away as the moon. Florida was the place all the retirees from up north came when it got cold, but not many chose this trailer park in Tallahassee. Tim couldn't blame them.

He ambled along the dusty road with his frayed backpack slung over his shoulder, kicking at rocks, watching school buses kick up more dust along the road. It was nearly a mile walk home, so he should have taken the bus, but getting there later was better than sooner. And Tim hadn't exactly become the most popular kid in the neighborhood. He'd actually tried to stay away from them. When he heard laughter behind him, he headed into the forest just far enough to let the kids on bikes pass.

Tim had been through a lot of changes in the past few months. He'd gone from being full-time on the road with his dad to full-time in school and living with distant cousins. They weren't distant enough.

His dad had done his best with school, but the way they both figured it, Tim had spent so much time around cars and motors that his future was there, so why fight it?

"As long as there are cars, they're gonna break down," his dad had said. "And then they need to be fixed. Job security. Whether it's with a crew like this or in some shop, you can do this the rest of your life."

Except the rest of his dad's life hadn't lasted long. At least not as long as Tim had hoped. Funny how he'd thought his dad would always be around.

A bunch of people had come to the funeral back in October, and there had been talk of some kind of benefit race for Tim that never happened. A few drivers, including the Overton crew, had given money to a fund, but Tim hadn't seen any of it. The media probably would have covered it more if they'd had video of the crash. The pit camera had cut out right before the accident. Go figure.

A nice car was parked near the trailer, right next to the wooden porch with all the peeling paint. Tim had seen the car before, but he couldn't place it. He stared at the license plate, but it wasn't until he looked in the backseat and saw two boxes of shoes and a weird-looking hat that it clicked.

Social worker.

The screen door squeaked, and his cousin Tyson's wife, Vera, stepped onto the porch with the woman. "Here he is now," Vera said with a drawl. Vera didn't pay much attention to Tim except when he was opening the refrigerator. She put sticky notes all over the food she didn't want him to eat, which was pretty much everything in the fridge except the milk.

"You walk all the way from school?" the social worker said. Her name was Lisa. He remembered that. Nice smile. Perfect skin. Tiny glasses that made her look older than she was. Probably in her 20s. Her voice was confident, and she walked like she owned the place, sticking out her hand for Tim to shake. She wasn't from the South—you could tell that by the way she talked.

"He doesn't like riding the bus much," Vera said.

Lisa stared at him. "You want to take a walk?"

Tim looked at her open-toed high heels. "You won't get very far in those around here."

She smiled, kicked them off, and pulled some Crocs out of her backseat. "You want to leave your backpack?"

Tim shook his head. "Not heavy."

They walked down the road by the trailer park and onto a path leading to a playground at the edge of the forest.

"Why don't you ride the bus?" Lisa asked.

"I like walking."

"What about school? You like it there?"

Tim shrugged. "It's okay, I guess."

"I talked with a couple of your teachers, and they said you were pretty quiet most of the time but that you're really smart."

"Why'd you talk to my teachers?"

She stopped and turned. "Tim, this is my job. I'm supposed to look out for you. Check on how you're doing. I'm not the FBI. I'm on your side."

They walked a little farther. Some kids on skateboards rattled along the concrete path to the playground. Smaller kids played on swings and slides, their moms hovering.

"How about home?" Lisa said. "You getting along okay with the Slades?" She chuckled. "What a name, huh?"

Tim smirked. "I guess I'm doing as well as can be expected."

"What's that mean?"

"I don't know. It's just hard living with people you've never known."

"Are they mean to you?"

"Define *mean*."

"Do they watch TV with you? eat meals together? yell at you? throw stuff at you?" She looked at his jeans. "Let you buy new clothes?"

"They're sorta tight on the finances."

"Tim, they're getting a check every month for the extra cost of taking care of you. That's supposed to go to food and clothes and school supplies."

"Maybe the check hasn't come yet."

Lisa sat on a bench and folded her arms. "I talked with your counselor too."

"Oh, boy." Tim sat directly across from her and watched the kids on the playground.

"He said you haven't been there in at least a month."

"I was kinda sick."

She leaned forward. "There's nothing that says you have to go to the counselor. Sometimes people don't want to talk about stuff that brings up bad memories. I can understand that."

"I'm not scared of memories. I just don't want to talk with that guy. Gives me the creeps."

"Why?"

"He's getting paid for talking to me. That's all we do. Just talk. Seems weird to me."

"Is that what your cousin said?"

Tim didn't answer.

Lisa sighed and hung her head. Finally she scooted to the edge of the bench. "Tim, you've been through the biggest change of your life. The counselor is there to help you through it. And I simply want you to have the best chance at life you can get."

"I'm doing all right. Don't worry about me."

She stood and walked toward a winding path around the playground. "Come on—let's keep walking."

He followed. A warm breeze blew through the palm trees, and a hint of moisture was in the air, as though there might be a thunderstorm coming. As Tim had learned, when a thunderstorm rolled in, you had to head inside fast.

"What about your dad?" Lisa said. "You miss him?"

"That's a dumb question."

"Yeah, you got me on that. I just didn't know how to bring it up."

Tim stuck his hands in his pockets. "I don't know. Dad probably wasn't ever going to win awards for best father or anything like that. I know some people thought I shouldn't be traveling with him and I ought to be in school. I learned a lot, though."

"Sure you did. And you probably wouldn't trade that time for anything."

"You got that right. If I'd have been somewhere in a school, I'd probably never have known him."

"What about your mom?"

"What about her?"

"She ever get in touch? Do you hear anything about her?"

"I haven't seen her since I was little. She left when I was in third grade."

"No letter? No contact at all? Didn't come to the funeral?"

Tim shook his head.

"Didn't you find anything about her in your dad's stuff?" Lisa asked. "An address? Phone number?"

"I never got to look at any of it. Tyson said they didn't have room for it here. They put it in some storage place over on Highway 27."

"And Tyson took your dad's truck?"

"Drives it to work. When his head's not hurting too much."

"Does he have a medical problem?"

"Yeah, it's called Budweiser."

"I see."

"I don't want to get him in trouble or anything."

"You won't. I just want a true picture, and I think I'm getting it. Your dad didn't leave a will or a trust. Could it have been in that stuff?"

Tim shrugged. "Almost everything he owned he carried in the truck."

"Maybe I can work it out for you to get access to his things."

"I'd like to see them."

They walked a little farther to a gravel path that led to a pier overlooking a lake. Some kids tried to skip rocks, but they just plopped in the water. There was movement beneath them, and Tim didn't like the look of those grayish green backs and the reptilian eyes on the water's surface.

"Season's starting again soon," he said. "Gonna be weird not going to Daytona."

"Have you heard from any of the crew? the guys you and your dad traveled with?"

"No. I guess they're busy getting new jobs. Overton retired after Homestead." They began the long walk back toward the trailer, and Tim picked up a rock and tossed it into the water. "You know, it's not so bad here. When I was out with my dad, I had about this much room I could call my own." He held out his hands. "Now I've got about 10 times the space. I get three meals a day and a bed. It's not the Hampton Inn, but it's all right."

"You don't have to protect them," Lisa said.

"I know. I just don't think they're the whole problem. Part of it's me."

"You?" Lisa said, her forehead creased in disbelief. "You're the one who lost your dad. You have a right to be ticked off at life."

"Yeah, but I'm not. I feel . . . I don't know. Kinda numb. Like I'm walking through some big mall, but all the stores are locked. I don't feel much about Dad except that I miss being on the road together. It's almost like all that was just a dream."

"It wasn't a dream, Tim. It was real. You two had a lot of good times. You did stuff kids can only dream about. I wish I had that kind of time with my dad when I was your age."

"What was he like?"

"This is supposed to be about you, not me." She bit her lip and stared at the setting sun. "He sold insurance. We moved about every year or two, so I'd make friends just in time to leave them. Kind of like a military family, I guess."

"He still living?"

"Yeah. He and my stepmom are out in Arizona. My mom died of cancer a few years ago."

"I'm sorry."

Lisa turned to him. "There's some stuff you don't know. Stuff I can't tell you yet. But there may be a way out of Apalachicola. If you had it, would you take it?"

They were a stone's throw from from the trailer

park. His dad's truck was in the parking space in front. Tyson was on the porch talking with Vera. When he saw them, he yelled, "Hey, I want to talk with you!"

"Would you want to leave here if you could?" Lisa said to Tim.

"Maybe," Tim said. "I'd think hard about it."

Tim's cousin stalked toward them, his boots cutting into the hard clay. He pushed his ball cap back on his head and dropped his hands to his sides. "He in trouble again?"

"No, this is just a social visit, Mr. Slade," Lisa said, flashing her white teeth.

"I told him he'd better shape up or we'd have to send him off to the home for waywards."

"No need for that. Tim seems like a pretty good kid. What kind of trouble?"

Tyson Slade's face was scarred. Tim figured it was bad teenage acne that had never been treated. He wore sunglasses too. Tim guessed that was so his employer couldn't see his bloodshot eyes.

"Some neighborhood kids don't care for him," Tyson said. "I wonder if he hasn't brought it on himself."

"And how would he do that?" Lisa said.

Tyson cocked his head, as if her tone wasn't appreciated. "Surely in your line of work you know how kids can be. They say something smart-alecky or get on people's nerves. One thing leads to another."

Lisa nodded. "Yeah, I know. Have a good day, Mr. Slade." She glanced at Tim. "I'll get back to you soon about your options."

Tyson looked at Tim after Lisa left. "What options was she talking about?"

JAMIE KNEW THE PREVIOUS year had not been good for her dad, Dale Maxwell—at least not in his sponsors' eyes. His best finish was ninth at Martinsville, late in the season. Some engine trouble two weeks in a row and crashes at Daytona and Darlington had severely hurt his earnings. Then there was Talladega.

Driving, as he had often told her, had been in his blood since he was a kid. His dad had told him that once he snapped the steering wheel in place, there was nothing he'd do that would even come close to the thrill of racing. It was a charge that would reach deep into his soul.

Her grandfather had been right about him, and it looked like the heart of her father beat in her, too. It wasn't that she wanted to prove she could make it in a guy's sport. It wasn't about a girl over-coming the odds. Jamie's passion was speed, and her eyes sparkled every time she talked about NASCAR or her car or anything that had four wheels. She didn't mind getting her hands dirty taking an engine apart. She never complained about the dirt of the tracks or the heat of the engine in the cockpit. She wondered if it was eerie for her dad to look at her—was it like looking in a mirror at himself, only with long hair and a pretty face? (At least, her dad said she had a pretty face.)

She had always been his partner when she was young, his "little helper" as he called her, going to the garage or to time trials, watching his every move. The whole crew marveled at how much she knew about the sport.

Now she could feel the distance. The older she got, the further she grew away from him. Because of his schedule during the season, he didn't come to many of her races—part of the reason she drove the Legend car. It was much easier for her mom to tow with just the Suburban. Jamie wondered if perhaps her dad couldn't stand the thought of his little girl get-ting hurt. Or maybe it was something else that made them grow apart.

Jamie knew she was perceived as all girl at school and church. Feminine. Petite. She could spend an hour with her hair on Sunday mornings, and she had good taste in clothes. But given the choice, she'd choose jeans and a T-shirt, tie her hair in a ponytail, and slap on a racing hat. That was her favorite out-fit—other than the fire suit.

She knew her dad was proud of her. Especially of how she'd handled Chad Devalon. Her dad had the same problem with Chad's father and said he dreaded seeing #13 in his rearview mirror.

"You ought to tell her how you feel," her mom had said to her dad one evening. Jamie was in the next room, listening. "She needs to hear what you think about her."

Words were difficult for her dad. He could stand in front of reporters and answer any question that came up with a wink and a nod and a smile. He could keep his cool after someone had bumped him into the wall with only a couple of laps to go. But the hardest thing in the world was talking to his teenage daughter. At least, that's how Jamie figured it.

TIM CARHARDT SQUEEZED through the narrow back window of his room, balancing on the thin railing that ran above the concrete behind the trailer. It was overcast, and a light rain had begun. His foot slipped, and when he reached back for the window, he cut his hand on the rusty siding. He jumped down—into mud—then crawled to a chain-link fence leading to the highway.

Tyson's voice boomed through the thin walls and out the back window. He banged on Tim's door and threatened to knock it down—kind of like the Big Bad Wolf, Tim thought. The guy even looked like a picture of a wolf in a book he'd read when he was a kid.

Tim's dad had also had a problem with the bottle years ago, but when Tim's mother left, there had been a change. Tim couldn't remember the last time he saw his father drinking beer or whiskey. He always told the other guys, "I'm a driver. I can't afford to get drunk."

Not so with Tyson. He missed work, got into fights, and smashed up his car all because he drank too much.

Something shattered inside. Sounded like glass. Vera wailed and cursed at Tyson.

Tim pulled the hat his dad had given him low on his forehead and took out a handkerchief to wipe his bloody hand. His dad always said that a gentleman should carry a handkerchief, and Tim had thought it was kind of a dumb thing to do, but he obeyed anyway. Now he was glad.

He let the rain wash the wound, then wrapped it tightly. He shoved his hands in his jeans and shivered in the chill. It was amazing how cold the rain could be, even in Florida. He wished he'd brought a jacket, but he hadn't wanted to spend another minute with Tyson on the other side of the door. Plus, he was on a mission. During a fight with Tyson, he'd discovered where the man kept the key to his dad's stuff.

He walked along the side of 263, seeing signs pointing to Florida State University. Just about every car that passed had a Seminoles sticker on the back. Nobody wanted to pick him up and get him out of the rain, but he couldn't blame them. If he were driving, he wouldn't pick up a wet rat like him either. He kept watch for Tyson in his dad's truck.

When the rain fell harder, Tim ducked under the cover of a convenience store awning. He stood between an ice cooler and some newspaper dispensers out of the rain. It was a winter rain without lightning that washed everything clean.

A car drove in slowly, backed up, then pulled forward to a pump. A white-haired woman got out and stared at the instructions on the front of the pump before finally sliding a credit card. A man sat behind her waiting, shaking his head, talking to someone on his cell phone.

When the woman fumbled with the gas cap, Tim walked through the rain to the island. "Need some help, ma'am?" he said.

She looked up like a frightened pup. "No, I can get it," she said, trying to convince herself.

Her fingers were gnarled and twisted, like Charlie Hale's, the hauler driver who used to work with Tim's dad. "Is it Mr. Arthur?" Tim said, pointing to the woman's hands. "That's what a friend of mine used to call it. Arthur-itis."

She smiled and let go of the gas cap. "There's a special way to get it off, and my husband could do it every time. . . ."

The man behind her rolled down his window. "You gonna talk all day or get some gas?"

"What a rude man," the woman said.

"Probably didn't have a good upbringing like you and me," Tim said.

She grinned. "Well, if you could just put $15 in, I'd appreciate it. Unleaded regular. Try not to go over."

Tim snapped off the cap, showing her how to turn it, then flipped up the lever and started fueling.

The man on the cell phone backed up and pulled into a space on the other side of the pump, grumbling, "Some old bat who shouldn't even be allowed to drive . . ."

"You live around here?" Tim said.

"I'm on my way back home. My daughter and her husband live down in Woodville. Do you work here?"

"No, ma'am. Just kinda hanging out till it stops raining." Tim let go of the pump at $14.78 and clicked it up to $15 even. He replaced the nozzle and the cap and noticed a drip underneath the car. He knelt and reached a long arm under the engine block.

"Is something wrong?" the woman said.

Tim saw his dad's truck slowly pass the station, and he stayed down. He held up a greasy finger. "Looks like antifreeze."

"Is that serious?"

Tim popped the hood. "The reservoir's almost empty, so you'd better get it looked at soon."

"What could it be?"

"Crack in the tank. Maybe the freeze plug worked loose—"

"The freeze plug! I just had one of those changed. At least that's what the fellow at the shop told me was wrong. He said I had a bad one."

The man with the cell phone slammed his door and sped off.

"Well, if they put it in crooked or didn't get it all the way in, that could cause the problem," Tim said. "If you want, I could fill it up for you so you don't run out before you get home."

"That's awfully nice of you."

She handed him a $20 bill, and he bought a gallon of antifreeze and topped off the tank. He handed her the change, but she said, "No, you keep it."

"I couldn't do that, ma'am." He stuffed the cash in her purse and put the antifreeze on the floor of the backseat.

"Well, you've been helpful. Is there anything I can do for you?"

The sky had begun to clear a little, but the rain was still coming. Tim's dad had always told him it was a bad idea to ever hitchhike, and he wouldn't have taken a ride from just anybody, but an old woman on her way home seemed safe to him. "To tell you the truth, I'm trying to get to a place on Highway 27. You're not going that far, are you?"

A cloud came over her face. She looked at Tim's wet clothes, then his hat. He stood a little straighter. "I'm sorry, but I have to be going."

Tim nodded. "I understand. You have a safe trip, ma'am."

He bought a Dr Pepper and waited. The rain slowed a little, and he figured if he didn't start walking now, he wouldn't make it home before midnight.

He was only a half mile from the store, crossing another parking lot, when a car swerved over, barely missing him.

The old woman rolled down her window and nodded to the passenger side. "You gonna get in, or are you going to swim to Highway 27?"

Tim got in, took off his hat, and put it on the floor.

"Buckle up, now."

"Ma'am, you don't have to do this."

"I know it, and you shouldn't be taking rides from strangers. There are some crazy people out here on these roads. You just never know about people these days."

"I could say the same thing to you. You shouldn't be giving rides to strange teenagers. What made you turn around?"

"The Lord."

"Excuse me?"

"Yeah. I got a strong impression from the Lord that he wanted me to give you a ride. A cup of cold water and all that."

"A cup of what?"

"I don't want to pass up the chance of entertaining angels, you know. In the Bible it says that some have welcomed angels by being kind to strangers."

"I can assure you, ma'am. I'm no angel."

"Well, neither am I, so we're even. Now where do you want to go?"

Tim pulled out a crumpled piece of paper and gave her the address.

"Land sakes, and you were going to walk? Must be gold in this place. What is it?"

He told her.

"A storage place? You bury treasure there?"

Tim chuckled. "It's just some stuff of my dad's I wanted to look at."

"Your father's away?"

"Yeah."

"Does your mother know you're out here?"

Tim hesitated, then turned to the woman. Her hands were wrapped tightly around the steering wheel, her eyes glued to the road. "You're not with the FBI, are you?"

"Goodness, no." She laughed.

"Good, because I was beginning to wonder. You must watch a lot of those police shows on TV."

The skin underneath her arm jiggled as she chuckled. "Well, the least you can do is tell me your name."

"Tim Carhardt," he said.

"I'm Mrs. Rubiquoy, but all my students used to call me Mrs. Ruby." She thought a moment. "You're not related to the Carhardts up in Opelika, are you?"

"Don't believe so, ma'am. Guess I could be and not know it."

She had a Christian music station playing with songs that sounded like they were a hundred years old and were going about as slowly as she was. He didn't know a car could go so slow. It was at least 10 years old, but the upholstery looked almost new.

"You were a teacher?"

"Librarian. Worked 26 years at Briarcliff Elementary until they had to lock the door on me."

"I doubt that."

"Well, every now and then I go back. You like to read?"

"Don't have much time for it with school and all. Just what they assign us."

"Hmm. Let me see." Mrs. Rubiquoy glanced at him, then squinted and maneuvered her mouth into a thin line. "You're probably reading *Great Expectations*. Or maybe *To Kill a Mockingbird*."

"Close," Tim said. "I'm a little older than I look. The teacher assigned us *The Old Man and the Sea* last week."

"Oh, what a marvelous story. You know, I always hated it when teachers would assign something and take all the fun out of it for the students. Tests and quizzes and such. I guess you have to do that to motivate them, but young people should learn that reading is fun. Don't you think reading is fun?"

"Sometimes I read the back of the cereal box, and that makes me laugh."

She clucked like a chicken, and Tim made a mental note not to make her laugh again because she nearly hit a light pole.

"Your husband hasn't been around for a while, has he?" Tim said.

"Died two years ago February. Traffic accident. He was coming home from a fishing trip and just swerved off the road. They said it was a heart attack, but I think it was because he was so excited to show me what he'd caught. They found the fish on ice in the trunk."

"I'm sorry."

"The Lord gives and he takes away. It's all for a purpose. But that doesn't make it easier late at night or when you read something and want to tell your husband about it and you realize he's not there."

Tim just stared at the road.

"What about you? You have a relationship with him?"

"I didn't know your husband."

"No, I meant the Lord."

Tim turned and looked out the passenger window. "God's never had much time for me, and I guess I returned the favor."

They came to a red light, and Mrs. Rubiquoy looked left to watch the traffic. Her purse was open beside her, and Tim noticed a $100 bill sticking halfway out.

"Now you keep an eye out for that storage place because it has to be up here somewhere."

They drove another mile before Tim spotted it on the right.

She pulled over and let him out. "The Lord knew you needed a ride, didn't he?"

"Yes, ma'am, I guess he did. And I thank you for your kindness. Now look after that antifreeze plug real soon." Tim got out but leaned back in before he shut the door. The woman had a concerned look on her face. "Everything all right, ma'am?"

She looked at her purse, then at him. "Let me give you some money to help you get back home."

"No way." He locked the door and smiled. "I'll be fine. You and the Lord just get home safe, okay?"

A MAN WHO LOOKED LIKE a grizzly bear opened the front gate and ushered Tim past barking dogs to a six-story building. It had broken windows and wooden floors and smelled like somebody's dirty laundry. Surrounding it were smaller buildings that resembled garages.

The man looked Tim up and down. "You don't look old enough to have a locker here. You gotta be at least 18."

"It's my dad's stuff. He passed last October, and I haven't been able to get here."

The man ran a hand through his graying mane and paused. "Your locker's on the fourth floor, all the way to the back."

Tim took the freight elevator to the fourth floor and walked by rows of what looked like locked cages packed floor to ceiling with boxes. A few doors were draped with covers, but most he could see in. Some had lawn mowers, gardening tools, and even motorcycles. Bikes hung from the ceiling, tool chests were shoved to the back, and a few had old car parts in them.

The hall was dark with only a few lights strung here and there. The bare bulbs made the whole place look eerie, as though there were white puddles of light every few yards.

He found his father's number and stared through the holes. While other lockers were packed full, there was only a bed frame, a mattress, and a few boxes here. He opened the lock and walked inside, the floor creaking. He pulled the mattress out, placed it near a puddle of light, and sat.

The first box clattered as he dumped old car parts and gadgets onto the floor. A generator. A side mirror. Nuts and bolts. Tire gauge. An old drill and a box of bits. Stuff his dad just couldn't bring himself to trash and Tyson evidently didn't want.

When he'd scooped all the debris up and put the pile back in the box, he moved on to the second, which was filled with papers and file folders. Numbers on a hospital bill. Tim's birth certificate along with his footprints. *Could my feet have ever been that little?* He poked through a pile of newspaper clippings—obituaries with faded pictures, lists of the dead and their families. People who had been gone so long that no one missed them anymore.

Tim took out a coffee-stained marriage license. His parents' names stared back at him. As if they'd always been together. As if nothing had happened between the time they signed this and now. He looked over the license, their names, the seal of the State of Florida, and the name of the pastor who had married them. It listed his father's full name, Martin Clancy Carhardt, and his mother's maiden name, Alexandra Lee Burton. He remembered his dad calling her Lexy when they were getting along, which wasn't very often.

He closed his eyes and tried to bring her face back, but it wouldn't come. Just a blur of an image, hazy in his mind—brown hair, nice smile.

He stuffed the pages back inside and turned to the next box. Pictures. Not in albums or arranged in any special way, just stacks of pictures in haphazard piles. People he didn't know. Places he couldn't remember. All lumped together like fishing worms in a tin can. He leafed through the ones at the top, many of them black-and-white, some stuck together. Toward the bottom they turned to color, and he finally found a few of his mother. His mom holding him wrapped in a hospital blanket. His dad asleep on a couch, with Tim asleep on his chest. His mother mugging for the camera with a stomach the size of a basketball. Tim in a Halloween costume—a sheet with two holes cut out for eyes.

Tim found a brown envelope and filled it with some pictures he wanted to take with him. He pulled the fourth box close and stared at it. He'd dreamed he might discover a videotape of his dad looking into a camera, telling Tim he loved him, assuring him that he'd make something of himself someday. But if his dad hadn't even put together a will, how would he have made a video?

He opened the box. Inside were a few books, some NASCAR magazines, and an autographed picture of the King, Richard Petty. That might bring some money on eBay. At the bottom were trophies and an old baseball glove. Tim opened it, put it to his face, and smelled the leather. Best smell in the world—right up there with the oil-and-gas smell of the garage.

The trophies were mostly third-place finishes in local races from his dad's hometown. They were ordinary. Even cheap. But of all the things he could keep, his dad had hung on to them. At some point in his life, had his dad dreamed of driving?

The magazines in the box had one thing in common: each featured the death of a celebrated driver. Some had been killed on the track. Others in airplane or helicopter crashes. It seemed strange that his dad had kept those issues, though he knew his dad had been at some of the races and venues where the drivers were killed.

Inside the magazines, Tim found other memorabilia—autographed pictures and programs, plus a few photos of famous drivers standing with his dad.

The only thing that surprised him was a spiral notebook at the bottom. He'd seen one like it in his dad's glove box, but he always thought he was just writing down mileage, oil changes, and stuff like that. He didn't expect to find a diary.

His dad hadn't been the most talkative man on the planet. On trips across the country, Tim had gone hundreds of miles without his dad so much as grunting at him. But here in the notebook, it looked like his dad had poured out his heart about a lot of things. The writing wasn't neat by anyone's standard (another thing Tim had inherited), but deciphering it made Tim feel a connection he hadn't felt in months.

I don't think I've ever seen Lexy any prettier than in the moments after Tim was born. I couldn't believe what a miracle a baby's birth is. I can only hope I'll be a good father to this boy. I'm so scared I'm going to mess things up just like my old man did. Maybe I

*can break the cycle. At least, I sure hope to
give it a good shot.*

Tim closed the notebook and cradled it to his chest. As he put his head back on the mattress, he shoved his bandaged hand into his pocket and felt the $100 bill and wondered what his dad would think.

JAMIE FELT THE JUICES of competition stirring at church that night. Funny how they could just come up. Not *exactly* like when she was racing but pretty close.

She'd been blindfolded and spun around a few times, then had to balance a raw egg on a spoon, walk to the center of the room, and drop it into a pot of water. Her teammates behind her were shouting directions, telling her when to walk straight, left, or right. The only problem was, there was another team trying to do the same thing on the other side of the room.

"Keep going straight!"

"Turn left, Jamie!"

"Five yards right in front of you."

"Which one?" Jamie said.

"Straight, Jamie!" It was Vanessa Moran, a new girl in town. "It's right in front of you."

"Stop!" someone yelled.

"Now! Drop it."

She couldn't tell if it was her group or someone else.

"Go, Jamie!" Trace Flattery yelled over the din. She could always tell his voice. It sounded like he had about a hundred marbles in his mouth when he talked.

Jamie bent a little and tipped the spoon. She heard a splat, then another, and groans rose from both sides of the room. She reached up and took off the blindfold. At her feet was a broken egg. Ahead of her stood Gary Edwards, a hulk of a guy who played defense on the football team and center on the basketball team. He stood over the pot of water, grinning from ear to ear, his egg on the floor.

"Why didn't you listen to us?" Vanessa said. "What a klutz."

"Okay, hold it down," Pastor Gordon said. "Good job, Jamie and Gary. Take a seat." The man was in his late 20s, newly married, and looked more like a model from one of those ads at the mall than a youth pastor. Theirs wasn't the biggest youth group in town, but Pastor Gordon had a way of getting kids involved. When more kids heard about it, Jamie felt sure they'd come.

"All right, Jamie, tell me what happened out there," Pastor Gordon said.

"Everybody was yelling so loud—I couldn't tell which ones were on my team and which ones were yelling at Gary."

"So you got mixed up by the voices?"

"Yeah. It's like they were all jumbled up together, and I didn't know which one to follow."

"So when you dropped the egg . . . ?"

"I thought I heard my team tell me to."

The kids around her groaned. First pick at the pizza was on the line.

"All right, how about you, Gary?"

"I listened for Jimmy's directions because he has the biggest mouth."

Laughter.

"I knew his voice would boom out over everyone else's. And he's on the basketball team, so I figured if he messed me up, I'd get him back during a game."

"You'd actually do that?" Jimmy said, incredulous.

"Knew I wouldn't have to."

"You were closer than Jamie, but you still didn't get the egg in the pot," Vanessa said.

"Close counts, doesn't it?" Gary said.

"We'll sort that out in a minute," Pastor Gordon said. "But this proves the point we were just talking about. See, in life, you're going to hear a lot of voices telling you what to do and not do. Who are you supposed to believe? Advice from over here might sound good, but it may be bad. And like this egg, your life might crash and break.

"Now suppose, since we're right in the heart of NASCAR country, that you were out there on the track listening to your spotter, but somehow the wires got crossed and you were actually hearing someone else's communication? Can you imagine what would happen if the voice on the other end of that microphone said to go low and there was a car there?"

Trace raised a hand. "You know what? I heard that happened once in an old Busch Series race at—"

Pastor Gordon smiled. "Let's save that one for around the table. Trace, why don't you read that verse printed on the handout."

Trace held up the crumpled piece of paper. "'My sheep listen to my voice; I know them, and they follow me.'"

"That's right," Pastor Gordon continued. "Jesus was talking to people about who he was. In fact, at the end of his answer to them, they actually picked up stones to kill him."

"What for?" Vanessa said. "Just because he mentioned sheep? Talk about prejudice."

A few people snickered.

"No, look at verse 30. Jesus says, 'The Father and I are one.' Those people knew that Jesus was saying he was *equal* with God. Now, who are the sheep he's talking about?"

Cassie Strower held up a hand. "Well, Jesus is known as the Good Shepherd, so I think that anybody who follows him is one of the sheep of his flock."

"Excellent," Pastor Gordon said.

"Good one, little miss sheepherder," Vanessa mumbled.

"The question is, how do you hear the Shepherd's voice over all the noise out there in the world?"

"You have to listen?" someone said.

"Spend time with the Shepherd so you really know his voice," another said.

"We had a dog once who went deaf," Trace said. "No, it's true. And the only way you could get him back to the house was to bang a bunch of trash cans on the back deck. He only responded to the vibrations."

"They should change the verse," Vanessa said. "'My dog hears me bang the trash cans.'"

When the laughter subsided, Pastor Gordon spoke again. "Those are all good answers . . . well, mostly . . . but the truth is, you have to be connected to the Shepherd to really hear his voice."

"What do you mean?" Gary said. "I don't get it."

"Jamie, come back up here."

Jamie stood and put on the blindfold again. Pastor Gordon turned her around a few times and let her get

her balance. She took a spoon and an egg and stead-
ied it.

"In a minute, I want you all to yell at the top of
your lungs. Give Jamie bad advice; tell her to go left
or right or stop. It doesn't matter."

"That's not fair," Trace said.

Pastor Gordon put something over Jamie's head.
Enclosed headphones. "Can you hear me?" he said
through a microphone as the kids began yelling.

Jamie nodded.

"All right, I want you to turn to your left. . . .
Good. . . . Now walk straight ahead about five
steps. . . . Good. A little to your right. That's it. You're
about a foot away from the pot, so take a half step
forward and lean over. Excellent. Put your spoon
out just a little. There. Now tip it over. . . ."

Applause and hoots broke out in the room as the
egg plopped into the water. Jamie took off her blindfold. Vanessa sat with her arms folded.

Jamie sat with Cassie Strower. They were both pepperoni people—opposed to the sausage crowd on the
other side. Jamie had told her all about the race in
Alabama, especially what happened at the end.

"Your dad pretty busy?" Jamie said. Cassie's father
was an engineer with Upshaw, one of the best teams
in town and known for building fast cars.

"They caught a design problem with the new engine right before Christmas, and they've been scrambling ever since. Don't tell anybody I said that."

"Your secret's safe. Anyway, knowing your dad, the flaw will probably just make it faster in the end."

Cassie nodded. "That's what usually happens. Something bad leads to something good . . . if you let it."

Jamie gave her *the look*. "You trying to tell me something?"

"Not really."

"You're thinking about the race with Chad."

"You're the one who brought it up."

"I swear, Cassie, it's tough being around you sometimes. It's like you've got some kinda halo around your head."

"Are you sure it's not my winsome personality?"

"Yeah. I'm sure."

Cassie took a huge bite of pizza and stared at Jamie.

"This is what I'm talking about!" Jamie said.

"I'm just eating," Cassie mumbled, smiling and laughing until a piece of pepperoni nearly came out her nose.

When they'd both settled down, Jamie said, "Honestly, what should I do about Chad? And don't ask me what Jesus would do."

"What do you want to do about him? I mean, you've raced him at every level. You two mix it up at the summer shoot-out. It's not like you can avoid him if you want to win."

"No, avoiding is not an option."

"Ever tried to talk to him?"

"Ever tried brushing an alligator's teeth?"

Cassie took another bite of pizza. "Just listen to the voice. The Shepherd is pretty good about guiding; don't you think?"

Suddenly Jamie got that old feeling. Like she was late to a party and had forgotten the present— and it wasn't a costume affair and she was dressed as the Sugar Plum Fairy. The old hit to the pit of the stomach.

Had she *ever* heard the Shepherd's voice? Was all this church stuff she'd been doing just an act?

WHEN LISA, THE SOCIAL WORKER, found out Tim had hitched a ride with someone, she scolded him and shook her head. After lecturing him about the dangers of doing such a thing, her demeanor changed, and she asked what he had found at the storage place.

Tim told her, and she said, "What did you do after you opened all the boxes?"

Tim shrugged. "Just looked through them. Read some stuff my dad wrote down."

"And you stayed in that storage place all night?"

"It was late. I didn't have a way back home. And I guess the guy at the front forgot about me. It was dark anyway." He looked up at her; the woman's mouth was open. "There was a mattress in there. A lot firmer than the one back

Chapter 8
Another Option

at Tyson's place. I think he pulled that thing out of the trash anyway. It smells funny."

"How did Tyson find you?"

"He put two and two together. Saw that the key was gone. He showed up the next day."

"What precipitated your leaving?"

"Ma'am?"

"Why did you leave in the first place?"

"We had a disagreement."

"About what?"

"Tyson wanted me to apologize to his neighbors, and I said I wouldn't."

Lisa took a sip of her double-espresso caffe mocha. "Apologize for what?"

"I kinda rearranged their mailbox."

"You have a reason?"

"Yeah. Not a real good one, but I had a reason."

"What did they do, look at you wrong?"

"No, the kids over there took my hat. Threw it in the mud."

"The one your dad gave you?"

Tim nodded.

Lisa sighed. "I thought you said it was going okay at Tyson's."

Tim pulled the top off his Big Gulp and took a drink of Mountain Dew. They were sitting at a picnic table in a park not far from his house. He crunched an ice chip and looked away. "Tyson said the next place I'd go was some home for wayward youth. That not even foster parents would take a 15-year-old with troubles."

"That's not true," Lisa said. "If it's a bad situation, I want to get you out of there. I may have another option for you."

"Somebody else who needs money on the side? Tyson sure doesn't use the money he gets for food, because the fridge is pretty empty except for his favorite beer."

She reached into her purse and pulled out an envelope. "I want you to hang tough with Tyson and Vera. It won't be much longer. Just try to stay out of his way. In the meantime, I want you to have these."

She handed him the envelope. It had something written on the front in a fancy cursive, so curly and flowing he almost didn't recognize his own name. "What's this?"

"Open it."

He took out four red and white tickets with *Daytona 500* written across the top. "You gotta be kidding me." Tim stared at the tickets. Four passes to the infield at Daytona. He could see some of his old friends. Catch up on the latest with the crews. Maybe even see Charlie Hale if the guy had gotten a job. "How'd you get these?"

"The people at NASCAR have good memories. The lady I talked with said any race you want to see, you're there. *If* you feel okay about going back into that world."

Tim smiled. "Better than the one I'm in right now. You want to go? You and your husband and somebody else?"

"I wish I could. And I'm sure my husband would kill me for turning you down. But I've got a trip scheduled that weekend. You have any problem getting over there?"

"I know the road like the back of my hand. Just hop on 10, turn right on 95."

"I meant, do you know who you'll go with?"

"Tyson would probably want to adopt me if he saw four tickets to Daytona." Tim laughed. "I don't think I'll let him know."

"Is there anyone from your school who'd like to go?"

"You kidding? Only about a hundred people. I'll be the most popular kid there."

JAMIE'S STOMACH CHURNED as she pulled into the parking lot of the Pit Stop, a tiny restaurant and lunch counter near the center of Velocity. Her 1965 Mustang chugged and sputtered after she turned off the engine. She'd have to put some additive in the gas tank to see if she could clean it out.

Jamie had bought the car from Mrs. Willits, one of her mother's friends, whose husband had died. She'd babysat for the family since she was 12. She spotted the car on cinder blocks in the Willits garage when she was 13. The youngest Willits boy had disappeared— something that happened at least once during each of her sitting jobs there. She'd run into the garage, looking for his hiding place, when she noticed a car covered with a gray tarp. She pulled it back, and it was love at first sight. She'd seen the model in magazines and at vintage car shows around town, but she'd never been this close to one. She opened the door, took one look at the black interior, and knew it would be her first car.

Jamie had made a deal with Mrs. Willits, trading a full year of babysitting along with $500 she had saved. She took possession of the car at 14 and began restoring the engine. Her dad helped in the evenings when he could and let her use his tools. She had to replace some upholstery and install a whole new brake system, but the main work was under the hood. With some help from a mechanic on the Maxwell team and a few volunteers from church, Jamie finished the car. When she got her driver's license, she'd driven away from the North Carolina Division of Motor Vehicles in Maxie, the name she had chosen for it.

Now, sitting in the parking lot, she couldn't believe how much money it took to keep a car going. Her dad paid the insurance, and she changed the oil herself, but she took care of all repairs, gasoline, tires, and registration. That, along with racing expenses, was why she accepted as many babysitting and house-sitting jobs as she could, along with her part-time job at the car-parts place.

But it wasn't the chugging of the car or the bills she was trying to pay that had her stomach churning. It was the sight of Chad Devalon's red Corvette

in the parking lot, only a few months old and spar-
kling like a diamond. His dad had bought it for him.
She'd heard it was because of his grades, but she had
a friend who went to the same private school he at-
tended and claimed Chad wasn't the brightest bulb
in the lighthouse.

Jamie had left a message on his cell phone and
asked for a meeting. She'd rehearsed what she was going to say a dozen times, but seeing that car brought
up the anger she felt.

Her other problem, of course, was that Chad was
undeniably cute. He was a jerk. He was despicable.
He wasn't a Christian. He was everything she didn't
want to be as a racer, but if you put all that aside, he
was hotter than the intake manifold on the 499th mile
at the Indy 500.

Jamie looked in her rearview mirror and took a
deep breath. She had to keep her head. She was on
a mission.

She spotted Chad sitting in the back as soon
as she walked inside. He wore a black jacket with
Devalon Racing in yellow letters, his back to the
door. His jet-black hair was squared in the back,
and he sat ramrod straight, though he occasionally
bobbed his head and tapped his foot to a country
song on the speakers.

"Hey, Jamie," the waitress said. It was Trace's

mother. "We're not very busy—you want a table or the counter?"

"I'm meeting someone, Mrs. Flattery," Jamie said.

The woman raised her eyebrows and looked at Chad. "You be careful now, you hear?"

Jamie nodded and walked to the booth. If Chad had been a gentleman, he would have taken off his hat and stood when she arrived. He did neither. All he did was look up at her with the straw of his strawberry milk shake sticking out of his mouth.

"Want one?" Chad said. "It's on me."

She shook her head. "I'm good."

"How'd you get my cell number?"

"I have connections, Chad. I'm not stupid."

"Nobody said you were stupid. What did you want to talk about?"

Mrs. Flattery walked by. "Can I get you something, Jamie? Shake? Bottle of Yoo-hoo?"

"Just a glass of water," Jamie said. Her mouth felt cottony, and she was having a hard time not being distracted by the song—it was one of her favorites.

"She's got to keep that figure of hers," Chad said. "Can't mess it up with sugary stuff."

"Give me that bottle of Yoo-hoo after all," Jamie said.

"Be right back," Mrs. Flattery said, winking.

"Listen, before you get started," Chad said, "about that Alabama race . . . I know you think I was being a jerk, trying to wreck you to get ahead. . . ."

"Yeah?"

"Well, I was just trying to win. Wasn't personal."

"Chad, every race we've run together has been personal. You've either been in front of me cutting me off or at my tail trying to bump me." She felt her blood pressure rising, her face getting hot. She grabbed the edge of the table, then let go when she saw he was watching her. "Why wouldn't I take it personally?"

Mrs. Flattery returned with a Yoo-hoo and a straw, scowling at Chad. "Here you go, honey."

"Well, I want you to know, it won't happen again," Chad said.

"Right," Jamie said. "Don't make promises you can't keep."

"I'm serious. I'm never running into you again. I'll never block you. You'll be safe on the track from now on."

Jamie shook the Yoo-hoo bottle and unscrewed the cap until it popped. As she stared at Chad, the song changed from bouncy to plaintive—a sad song about somebody crying and sitting by a fire, missing someone who had just walked out.

"So what is it *you* wanted to talk about?" Chad said.

"No, back up. Start over. Why are you saying this? You get religion or something?"

Chad laughed, and Jamie felt a jolt she hoped was the effects of the Yoo-hoo. His smile flashed like a missile on a radar screen. "I'm just saying I won't be a problem for you anymore."

"And how can you make that promise?"

"I'm moving up."

She almost choked, and she was just glad the Yoo-hoo didn't come out her nose. "You're what?"

"After that last race Dad thought I was ready to move up to Grand Nationals. We've been talking about it for a while. So he bought me a new car. But instead I'm going into a new division with better sponsors and tracks. Bigger purses too. I'm practicing next week if you want to come watch."

Jamie's heart sank. It was bad enough racing against Chad. The only thing worse would be watching him move up to another class and leave her in the dust. She'd talked with her dad about the possibility of moving up, but he said it was expensive and that she could learn all she needed where she was. She felt like tossing her drink on Chad's black jacket. Especially with that smarmy smile of his.

"He bought you a car?" Jamie said.

"One of the Devalon team members had one. Dad surprised me with it."

"Must be nice," she muttered.

"It's in perfect condition. It's in the shop now getting a fresh coat of paint. We'll need a backup, of course, but that can wait."

"If it was perfect, why paint it? Let me guess. Black?"

"You got it."

"Wait a minute. You smack into me and ruin my chances to win, and your dad says you're ready to move up?"

"That and what happened afterward. He said if I could keep my cool when a girl started throwing punches, I was ready."

"I never threw a punch. And you didn't keep your cool."

"I did enough for him."

"Don't you have to qualify?"

"With my record and the fact that I have a sponsor, Dad says I'm in. Plus, he knows some people."

Of course. Jamie's mind swirled. She leaned forward, elbows on the table. "How much does it cost? I mean, other than the car. What kind of fees do you have to pay?"

Chad told her, and her heart sank even further. She wanted to scream. Since she'd seen her first NASCAR race, she'd dreamed about becoming a driver. At 10 she'd set a goal but hadn't told a living soul about it.

It was her dad who had nailed it when he asked why she wanted to spend all her time at the kart track. She'd hemmed and hawed until he pressed her again. "Because I'm going to be the first girl to win the cup, Dad," she'd said.

Her dad had smiled and patted her head. "I just bet you'll do it."

Jamie drained her Yoo-hoo and dropped two dollars onto the table.

"So, no hard feelings?" Chad said, putting out a hand.

She shook his hand and left without saying a word.

TIM DIDN'T HAVE WHAT he would call a real friend in high school. The past few years, when he lived on the road, his only friends had been the crew guys who actually talked to him. And his dad.

There were a few guys he knew from classes who would say hello to him, plus Kimberly, a girl on the student council ambassador program. On his first day, she'd showed him to his locker and given him a tour of the school. She'd asked what groups he was interested in joining.

Tim just shrugged. "You got a NASCAR club?"

"I know there're a lot of people who watch it," she said. "There are a bunch of them in my youth group. You ought to come to our church—the group meets on Tuesday nights."

Tim scratched his head. "I'm not really into religious stuff."

"Well, keep it in mind. It's a good way to meet new people."

He'd seen Kimberly in the hall a few times after that. She'd waved and smiled, asking if he'd settled in okay and if he was having any problems with his teachers. Always remembering his name. She told him to sit in front in English and he'd get a better grade.

Who was he kidding? He hadn't been to school since his dad had taken him on the road with him. He didn't have any idea what most of the teachers were talking about. He'd done some workbooks in math and reading, but he'd basically fallen through the cracks after his dad sold their house.

He carried his father's notebook to class and read sections of it when he was supposed to be listening or taking notes. It wasn't as though his dad had been William Faulkner or Herman Melville, a couple of guys his English teacher had talked about. The stuff his dad wrote was often just scribbled notes or thoughts about the team or his frustration with his life, but it was intensely personal to Tim. It was like living alone on an island and suddenly finding a pen pal. Although he couldn't write to this pen pal.

I'm worried about Lexy. Today she called and sounded really sad. Said she felt like she couldn't care for Tim anymore. Needed some space.

I made some joke she didn't laugh at, then told her we'd talk when I got home. She just started crying. Tears my heart out when I hear that. Worst feeling in the world. I wish I could bring them both out here with me, but I can't.

The bell rang and Tim piled his stuff in his backpack. When he got to the hall, he saw Kimberly and caught up to her. She smiled and asked a billion questions about his classes and if he'd made friends and all that.

When he could get a word in, he said, "You said you know some people who are interested in NASCAR. Can you think of anybody who might want to go to Daytona in a couple of weeks?"

"That's a big race, isn't it?"

Tim nodded.

"Let me make a phone call or two. Or you could just come to our outing tonight. We're going bowling."

Tim recognized the bowling alley's name. It was about a mile from his house. "Okay, I'll meet you there tonight."

"YOU DID WHAT?" Jamie's dad said. His hands were dirty, and he had his hat pushed back on his head so it was sticking straight up at the ceiling. Jamie couldn't help noticing that his hair had grown grayer around the edges, and she wondered if that was from the racing or if part of it was her fault.

"I wrote an ad about my Legend car and put it in the paper."

"How'd you do that?"

"I did it online. And I'm thinking about advertising Maxie too."

"Wait, if you're giving up racing, why are you—?"

"I'm not *giving* it up. I'm *moving* up. There's a new division with better sponsors and tracks. Bigger purses too."

"Jamie, we've talked about this. I don't think you're ready. And there's no way we can afford—"

"Dad, the only race you've been to lately was Alabama. How would you know if I'm ready?"

"You know this is a busy time when we're getting ready for the season."

"Chad's moving up, and he's—"

"Is that what this is about? Chad and his dad? We don't live our lives or make decisions based on the Devalons. And to be honest, I'm glad to see you get away from him. He's dangerous."

"I'm not doing this because of Chad. I'm ready, Dad. I know it. You won't stop me from selling my car, will you?"

"Maxie is part of you, Jamie. Why would you want to sell her?"

"Because there's no way I can get enough money for the fees and a new car. Maxie will get me enough for the fees, and then if I can get a sponsor . . ."

He sighed heavily and walked into the kitchen.

Jamie followed him and found her mother listening to the conversation but staying out of it. She was busy with something on the stove, and Kellen sat at the kitchen table, bouncing his pencil on his math book.

"She's ready, Dad," Kellen mumbled. "I hate to admit it, but she is. You ought to let her move up."

"I don't need your input right now," he snapped.

"Keep working on him," Jamie whispered to Kellen.

Her dad washed his hands and ripped a paper towel from the dispenser. He just kept walking away, and usually Jamie would let him go, but for once she followed.

"Why do you have a problem with this?" Jamie said. "You've always told me to go after my dreams. To take chances when they come my way. I want to do this, but instead of being behind me, you're the one in the way."

"That's not fair and you know it." His face was red. "I've been behind you every step, but I can't just put my problems on a shelf and forget them." He walked into the pantry, then back into the kitchen and pulled out a chair. "One of my problems is how fast this came up. You've been fine right where you are. Learning, going faster, winning more. You seemed content racing your Legend car. What changed?"

"I've learned a lot, but I want to learn more."

"Nothing wrong with that," he said. "But it feels like you want to move up because Chad is."

"Okay, when I heard it, some feelings got triggered, sure. But you know what I've wanted to do since I was little, Dad."

"And I want to help you get there."

"You want to block me! You want to bang my bumper and spin me out."

"Nice metaphor," Kellen said.

They both looked at him like he was a boll weevil in a cotton field.

"There's nothing I'd like better than to help you reach your goal," her dad continued. "But I don't want you in a situation where you'll get hurt and have all your dreams crash."

Jamie hung her head. The old you'll-hurt-yourself-and-I-care-too-much-for-you-to-let-that-happen answer. She hated that answer. "If I were a boy, you wouldn't be saying this."

"True," Kellen said.

"All right, you are out of here," her dad said, picking up Kellen's book and tossing it onto the couch in the living room. "Go. Now."

Kellen walked away like a dog that had just had an accident on the carpet. "I'm just trying to be a good brother."

Her dad leaned against the island, where her mother was still stirring. Why wasn't she getting into this?

"Jamie, you have great reflexes—you're a natural at driving. I couldn't be any prouder of you for what you've done. I just want you to be ready."

"Is this what your dad said to you?"

He took off his hat and held it in front of him, chuckling. "My dad was old school. He'd hop in a car and hope. Just mash the pedal to the floor and see how fast and how far he could go. Racing's a lot different today—you know that."

"Yeah, but he encouraged you, didn't he? He let you move up when you wanted."

The phone rang before he could answer.

Kellen raced them to it and answered. He handed the phone to Jamie. "It's somebody asking about your car."

AT FIRST, TIM THOUGHT the bowling alley was closed because it looked dark inside. There were cars in the parking lot, so he went inside and saw glowing pins and flashing laser lights. The music was loud but not loud enough to drown out the sound of falling pins. He loved that sound.

He couldn't believe he was actually going to a church function. That it was held here made it a little easier to stomach, but the whole thing made him uncomfortable. He wasn't very good around girls—especially the pretty ones—and he stood for a long time and looked at the lanes to see if he could find Kimberly. The guy behind the counter stared at him, probably wondering if he was going to rent shoes or not. Tim decided to leave.

"Hey, you did come!" Kimberly said

behind him. She had an order of nachos that looked like it would feed an army. She offered him some, and though he was starving, he shook his head. That was something else he couldn't do in front of pretty girls: eat.

"We're over on the first six lanes. Grab some shoes and meet us."

Tim walked to the counter and told the man his size.

"I've got a pair of 9s and a pair of 10s, but no 9½s," the man said.

"Give me the 10s." He fished in his pocket. "Can you break a hundred?"

The man pointed to the sign above his head. No bills larger than $20. "But if you're with that group, the church pays for the whole thing. Never seen you in here before."

"My first time."

He handed Tim the shoes. "They call them the Holy Rollers. Get it?"

Tim smiled. "Yeah, that's a good one."

The kids didn't look like what Tim expected. He thought they'd be wearing ties and suits and have halos. Instead, they wore jeans and looked normal. *Probably just to throw me off*, he thought.

Kimberly introduced him to the youth leader,

and Tim shook the man's hand. He looked normal too.

Tim didn't bowl well because he'd done it only a few times. When he did keep the ball out of the gutter, he knocked down just a couple of pins. After a game, he sat out and watched.

"This is Jeff," Kimberly said about an hour after Tim arrived. "He's a huge NASCAR fan."

Jeff wore a NASCAR hat and jacket and shook Tim's hand firmly. People at churches sure seemed to shake hands a lot. Jeff suggested they go to the restaurant to talk. It was a lot quieter.

"Never seen you in school," Tim said.

"That's because I don't go to your school." He told Tim where he went. "What do you think of the group?"

"It's all right, I guess," Tim said.

"Yeah, it's kind of lame when the guy talks, but there're a lot of girls. Gotta go where the action is, you know?"

"Yeah."

"So, Kimberly said you have some tickets?"

"I've got three pit and garage passes if you're interested."

"Interested? You bet. How'd you get them?"

"I know some people."

"Wow, pits and garage. How much you want for them?"

"I'd give them to you if I could get a ride down there. I don't have any way to the race."

"Free tickets just for a ride?" Jeff laughed and slapped Tim on the shoulder. "That's awesome. What day?"

"Sunday. The cup race."

"Awesome," Jeff said, smiling. "You're as good as there, my man." He shook Tim's hand again.

Simple as that. Give away some tickets and everything would work out. Tim was on his way to Daytona.

THE CALL WAS FROM a kid who asked a few questions, then hung up. *Probably has no cash,* Jamie thought.

She and her dad continued talking, and the discussion became more and more heated.

With tears in her eyes, Jamie said, "You know I've dreamed of this since I was little. Why are you doing this to me?"

"I don't expect you to understand," her dad said, his own eyes misting. "But you've gotta believe me when I say that I want you to succeed even more than you do. That's why I think it's best to wait."

"You can't stop me from selling Maxie," she sobbed.

"No, and I won't. You want to sell it, go ahead."

"And my car."

"If you want to raise the money early, I'm okay with that. But you won't have anything to drive."

Jamie smacked the wall. "I wish I was Grandpa's girl and not yours!" She knew it wasn't fair. She knew it wasn't true. But she said it anyway because she knew it would hurt him. Sometimes, when she hurt the most, it was the only thing she could think to do. But it never helped. It always felt like those big sandwiches she saw wrapped up in the cooler at Wal-Mart. They *looked* really good, but when she ate them, she got a weird feeling in her stomach. What looked good didn't really satisfy.

She spent that night writing up the best ad she could come up with for Maxie.

> *Fully restored 1965 Mustang 2+2 Fastback.*
> *It has a 289 2V and C4 transmission with*
> *less than 100K miles on it. What a beauty.*
> *The engine is the original, rebuilt by owner.*

When she finished, she stuck the ad in the top drawer of her desk and went to sleep. She dreamed of making the last turn at Daytona, fending off Chad, and taking the checkered flag.

/////

The Maxwells had a family tradition Jamie loved, though she would never tell them or show them that. She and Kellen would take a few days off from school, and they'd all drive to Daytona, pulling the camper the family had bought after her dad placed 15th at Darlington. Jamie had heard about the early days of NASCAR when families would go to church in the morning and to the racetrack in the afternoon. The mom would spread out a picnic lunch while the kids played on the infield, and then they'd eat fried chicken or hot dogs during the race. When it was over they'd head home (assuming the dad hadn't crashed the car). The sport was purer back when her dad was a kid, but the drivers were poorer.

Jamie and Kellen leveled the camper using bricks while their mom went to the drivers' meeting to find their dad. A section of the infield held the drivers' massive RVs that dwarfed the Maxwell setup. Jamie felt puny next to them and more than a little jealous. If her dad could actually win a couple of races, maybe they could afford to at least *rent* something like that. Many families actually lived on the road from February through November, but Jamie's parents had decided to give their kids as normal a family life as they could. That meant Dad was gone a lot, and they had to watch his races on TV most weekends, except during the summer.

Jamie zigzagged through the RVs, walking toward the track as the February Florida sun beat down. She liked living in a place with four seasons, but she could see herself living somewhere like this—or maybe California—one day.

Jamie knew that most people would never get to experience the excitement of race preparations like those in the garage and pits. Stacks of Goodyear tires were lined up from the midpoint of the backstretch all the way to the first turn, and teams scrambled to find their lot, using dollies to bring them back to the garage. Each team had a small space for their car inside and outside the garage, a long building with separate bays in the middle of the track. Semi trucks parked side by side and unloaded cars before the race. If someone failed to qualify for the race, they'd have to pack their stuff and move out. It was kind of like not being chosen for a game of pickup basketball, only with a lot of money on the line.

Jamie had seen families leave in tears. In fact, she had experienced it herself, but fortunately her dad had never failed to qualify at Daytona. This was one of his favorite tracks.

The smells of charcoal and sizzling burgers and bratwurst made her mouth water. Some drivers (and teams) were successful enough to hire their own chefs. Others had a motor coach driver serve as cook.

She leaned against the white wall. In a couple of days this site would be filled with crews in fire suits ready to help their driver win. She closed her eyes as a driver went into a practice run, imagining herself inside the cockpit. *Someday, if I can ever convince Dad, that's going to be me,* she thought. *Someday I'm going to take the checkered flag here. Someday those stands will be filled with people with my number on their hats. And Daytona will be only the beginning. When I pull into Homestead, I'll have the cup sewn up.*

There was an eerie feeling to the empty stands. Thousands of seats would be filled with cheering fans soon. But her thoughts roamed to the ghosts of Daytona—racers who had made this track their playground and were now gone. Each new generation of racers made their sacrifices worth it. As her dad liked to say, "We race on the backs of the giants."

"Jamie," someone said behind her.

She turned and caught her breath. "Chad."

"I saw you guys pull in from up there." He pointed behind him to a black bus that looked as big as a mountain. It was parked about a football field away, on the other side of the infield, and seemed to hover over all the other RVs. Above the coach were several antennas and a platform. From the infield, most families could see only a portion of the track, so they watched it on television and kept their doors open to hear the sounds of the crowd and the cars.

"We just fired up the grill," Chad said. "You should join us for lunch."

"I'm watching my little brother right now."

Chad looked around. "I don't see anybody."

"He's back at the camper."

"Well, bring him along."

"Holy Taj Mahal," Kellen muttered when he and Jamie walked toward the coach.

"Just act normal," Jamie said.

"How can I act normal when the TV in there looks five times as big as the one we have at home? Why are we going, anyway? You hate Chad."

"Let's see how the other half lives," Jamie said. "It's how I'm going to live one day."

"Really? You going to win the lottery?"

"Funny," Jamie said.

The motor coach smelled newer than a car show-room. It had carpet so deep it felt like she was wading through it. Captain's chairs lined a wall on the other side of the TV. The latest navigation and video—which looked like something NASA had developed—were available to the driver. The kitchen had dark, granite-like counters that were as shiny as mirrors. Same for the stainless steel appliances. Along the left side of the front room was a table spread with a fine white tablecloth. Finger sandwiches were placed carefully on silver platters, along with shrimp, stuffed mushrooms, vegetables and dip, and other stuff Jamie had never seen before, let alone tasted.

"Only thing this RV needs is a moat outside," Kellen whispered. "Get a load of those skewers with chicken and beef. And are those oysters? It's like eating at a king's castle without having to worry about wearing a suit of armor."

"Hello there, Jamie," a deep voice said. Butch Devalon walked through a curtain from the back hallway. Jamie could only imagine what the bedrooms were like. And the bathroom. Butch Devalon wore his fire suit, dark sunglasses, cowboy boots, and a black hat. He looked like a gunslinger in one of those old Westerns, except he didn't have a gun. "Chad told me you were coming. Burgers are cooking in the back. Welcome to our home away from home."

"Sure is a nice place," Jamie said.

Kellen picked up a shrimp as big as his hand. "Nice doesn't even begin to describe it."

The man chuckled and sat on a couch that creaked as he took off his boots and laced up his racing shoes. "Bet you're glad you won't be going up against Chad anymore."

"Oh, she's—"

Jamie cut her brother off. "I enjoy competition a lot, Mr. Devalon. Your son always . . . pushed me to do my best."

"Did he now? That's putting a positive spin on it. You looked a little ticked at the last race."

"I was upset at first, but that's racing." If she'd heard that line once on SPEED TV, she'd heard it a thousand times.

Mr. Devalon shook his head. "You're just like your old man."

"Nothing wrong with that," Kellen said.

Mr. Devalon smiled. "'Course not. If you want to stay in the back of the pack."

Jamie's blood pressure began to rise. Most drivers couldn't say enough good things about her dad. He knew when to be aggressive, but he was fair. In fact, he had one of the best reputations of anyone in NASCAR. You never had to guess about Dale Maxwell's character or where he'd stand on an issue. And you never had to wonder if he was going to do something dirty to you.

But Butch Devalon was another matter. Always locked in controversy. Arguing with other drivers. Even his own teammates didn't like dealing with him. He'd alienated just about every driver at one point or another.

"No, I think your dad's more concerned about being nice than he is about winning," Mr. Devalon continued. "The whole God thing doesn't mix with racing. It takes away all your competitive juices."

Jamie wanted out of the motor coach. She couldn't stand the sound of the man's grating, gravelly voice.

"I wonder if that's genetic," he said.

"What do you mean?" Jamie said.

"If the way a man drives is passed down to the next generation." He took a handful of macadamia nuts from a bowl on the table.

Jamie turned to the front door. She could say her stomach hurt or she wasn't really hungry. Kellen would probably protest and say he was starving.

But what Mr. Devalon said next snapped her to attention. "Some guys on my team have been talking about you."

Jamie squinted. "Me? Why've they been talking about me?"

"Probably heard how bad you did on your last math test." Kellen laughed.

Jamie flicked his ear but kept her gaze fixed on Mr. Devalon.

"One of the Devalon owners was at the track that night in Alabama. He's got a good nose for new drivers, and he said he thought you might have what it takes."

Jamie's eyes grew wide. She didn't know what to say.

Mr. Devalon went on. "Now I won't blow smoke

at you. I don't think females can go very far in this sport. Don't think they have what it takes physically *or* mentally. But he seems to think it's good for attendance to get 'em suited up. Makes the female fans happy, you know. Diversity and all that. I can pretty much guarantee you a woman'll never make it to the top 10, let alone win a cup. But then, there're a lot of people who'll never do that. Like your dad."

Jamie tried to ignore the digs against her father, but they kept coming.

Before she could say anything, Kellen said, "Why do you hate our dad so much? Are you jealous?"

Mr. Devalon pushed his hat up and spread both arms like a hawk on the back of the leather couch. "What's there to be jealous about? You guys have a ride like this? Has your dad won a race in the last two years? Or has it been three?"

"No, but life's more than the stuff you buy or always coming out on top," Kellen said.

"So, you're the philosopher in the family. That's good." He crossed his legs. "No, I don't hate your dad. I just don't think he belongs on the track. He's a goody-goody. The Lord this and the Lord that. Seems to me he shouldn't blame the Lord for his poor performances—he should blame himself. And he ought to turn his little girl loose, who's probably a better driver than he'll ever be."

Jamie stepped forward, ignoring what he'd said about all women and her dad. "What does your owner think I should do?"

He raised his eyebrows. "Shane told me he's thinking about signing you up. He'd probably throw a little money at you, move you into a car. This is off the record, of course. No promises. He's the kind of guy who can change his mind in about three seconds. And there's another potential opportunity—"

"What about Chad?" Jamie interrupted. "If this guy is so all-fired ready to sign people up, why wouldn't he sign your son?"

"Chad's in a different situation. We don't have as much financial pressure as you and your family. I'll help him along, and he can move up through the ranks. But someone like you . . . well, you need the extra help. And with the push to bring in minorities and women, you might just make it."

Jamie knew exactly what he meant. She'd heard about it before. A team signed an up-and-coming driver for a little money, gave him (or her) enough to keep him happy and racing for the team, and in a few years, if the new driver moved successfully through the competition, he could move up. It was a one-in-a-thousand chance the owner was taking, but if the man found a great driver, it would be well worth spending the cash.

Chad walked in from the back just as Jamie's cell phone rang. "We're pulling some burgers off the grill. You're staying, right?"

She answered the phone, then hung up. "That was my mom. We have to get back."

"Go ahead and take some food," Mr. Devalon said. "We've got more here than we could possibly eat."

Kellen grabbed a plate, but Jamie took him by the elbow. "Thanks, but we have to be going."

On the way back to their camper, Jamie made Kellen promise he wouldn't say anything about what he had heard.

"Why? You afraid Dad won't let you sign with them?"

"I just don't want them knowing, okay?"

"Fine. But you should've let me bring some of those shrimp. Mom would kill for those."

"WHERE YOU THINK YOU'RE going?"
Tyson said as Tim walked onto the front
porch of the trailer. Tyson wore just his
boxers and an old T-shirt.

Tim hadn't been able to sleep—he
was so excited to get to Daytona. And
with all the noise Tyson had made the
night before, drinking and playing cards
with his friends, he'd figured the man
would sleep until noon. "I told you guys
I'd be gone today."

"Where?"

He could have kept it to himself, but
there was something that made him
want to let Tyson wallow in his misfor-
tune. "Going down to Daytona."

The man's eye twitched, and a real
look of understanding came over him.
"Why didn't you tell me you wanted to
go? I'd have taken you."

"It's okay."

Chapter 14

"Who you going with?"

"A friend."

"I don't think that's a good idea. I'm gonna get dressed and drive you down there myself."

"I only got one ticket," Tim lied.

Tyson cursed. He walked back inside and paused at the doorway, as though he was going to say have a good time or something like that. But he just cursed again and shut the door.

Jeff pulled in an hour late in a red SUV. He had some grunge band on the radio that he had to yell over. The kind of music Tim really didn't care for, especially this early in the morning. It wasn't the words or how loud the guitars were or anything like that—it was that he couldn't understand it. Maybe he'd been traveling with his dad a little too much and his love of country music had rubbed off.

"I'll have you get in the back when I pick up the guys," Jeff said.

"Yeah, sure."

They made two stops, and Jeff had to go in and basically drag the guys from their beds. The first guy, Gavin, looked more like a string bean than a human being, and his hair stuck straight up in the back. If Jeff hadn't introduced him, Tim would have called him Gus, short for Asparagus.

Pete and Ian climbed in next. Pete had the longest nose in the history of teenagers and wore a #8 hat that looked a hundred years old. Ian bore a striking resemblance to a young Keanu Reeves, with dark hair and a face Tim figured girls swooned over. Somehow he seemed out of place with this group.

Pete had climbed into the front with a cooler, and it didn't take him long to open it and pop the top on a can of beer. "Who wants some?"

Tim shook his head—not because he'd never had beer but because it was so early. In fact, he'd had his first when he was 13, sneaking three from Charlie Hale's fridge. He'd finished the first one before he got sick. His dad had talked with him and then taken off his belt. "This is going to hurt me more than it will you," his dad said. Tim didn't believe it. His dad had a talk with Charlie after that, and he kept the fridge locked. The other guys laughed when they saw Tim the next day, but his dad's face had remained grim for a week. Tim couldn't help feeling he'd let him down.

Pete handed Tim a Coke. "I still can't believe you're just giving us tickets."

Tim shrugged and opened the red top. It had a black mark on it, as though someone had used a permanent marker to show the price. "It's a fair trade. Tickets for transportation."

Pete wiped beer foam from his mouth. "Hey, have

any of you guys actually seen these tickets? He's probably just pulling our leg. I'll bet he's got one ticket, and he's taking us along for the ride."

Tim pulled the tickets out of the same envelope Lisa had given him and handed them over.

Pete whooped and hollered, waving them around like he was holding a million dollars. "You're looking at pure gold here, boys. Pure gold." He winked at the others.

It took Tim until they passed the Live Oak exit to get up the nerve to ask why there were five of them and only four tickets.

Tim looked in the rearview mirror and saw Jeff's eyes locked on his, as though he'd anticipated the question. "Ian's going to buy one from a scalper outside. His family's in a different tax bracket than the rest of us."

Ian shook his head. "Don't believe him. My dad doesn't make any more than your parents. We moved here from California, so we got a bigger house. That's all."

Tim checked his watch. He couldn't remember being on this side of the race—driving to it instead of already being there. He'd always just gone with his dad and been there from the moment the truck parked. He knew it was important to get there early to find a parking place, especially if they were headed to the infield. You wanted time to mingle and actually see some of the drivers.

They rode with windows down, music blaring, wind whipping through the SUV, and the smell of suntan lotion Ian had slathered all over his arms and face. They took the exit from 10 to the 295, which skirted Jacksonville, and Tim downed the Coke.

It wasn't until they reached the exit for National Gardens that Tim felt the pain in his gut. He stuffed the plastic Coke bottle into the mesh holder in front of him and wrapped his arms around his stomach.

"You okay?" Ian said.

"Yeah, I'll be all right."

But he wasn't. His stomach rumbled and churned so much that he had to close his eyes and lean against the door. It felt as if his insides were knotted and wrapped like a water hose just tossed by the corner of a house. He couldn't listen to anyone talking, and he had to shut his mind off from the music. All he could think of was his stomach and the pain and how he couldn't wait to get to a bathroom.

Tim hadn't had any breakfast, so he couldn't have gotten food poisoning. He'd eaten some leftover fried chicken for dinner the night before, but that was a long time ago. What could have made him feel this bad?

"How much farther?" Tim said.

Pete turned. "Another couple of exits. You don't look so good, Tim. You feeling okay?"

The others laughed.

"I think I need to go to the bathroom."

"We need some gas," Jeff said. "We can get off at the next exit, okay?"

"Yeah, that'd be good."

Tim was well acquainted with gas station bathrooms. He knew there were good ones, bad ones, and ones you just turned around and left no matter how bad you needed to go. This one was the third category. It looked like it hadn't been cleaned in a year. He'd been in Porta Potties that smelled like a summer field compared with this place. But he couldn't be choosy. He staggered into a stall.

A few minutes later he tried to wash his hands, but there was no soap and no paper towels in the dispenser, so he wiped his hands on his pants. When he got to the door, another pain hit, and he had to run back to the stall. He slipped on the wet floor and nearly fell but made it inside.

He figured one of the guys would check on him, but it was enough that they waited as long as they did. He finally walked out into the sunlight, expecting the guys to clap or hoot and holler.

A family with every inch of the car stuffed with

people or suitcases fought at the first pump. Two girls ran past him to the women's room. A man covered with dry cement stood by a contractor's truck, the back filled with tools and buckets. Inside a convertible sports car, the top down, sat a woman with long brown hair and sunglasses that probably cost more than all the money Tim had in his pocket. He saw lots of cars and people but no red SUV.

He walked all the way around the station, then across the street to check out the McDonald's, thinking Jeff and the others might be waiting there. He went inside the convenience store, where one cashier tried to keep the line moving.

"Can I help you?" she snapped when he made it to the front of the line.

He picked up a Moon Pie and handed it to her, though the thought of a Moon Pie after what he'd just been through turned his stomach. "Did you see a red SUV with four guys in it? In the last half hour or so?"

She passed the Moon Pie in front of the scanner, and it blipped. Without looking up from the register she said, "Lotta cars came through here in the last half hour. That's $1.34."

He thought of trying to describe Jeff or Asparagus Head, but a guy behind him sighed heavily, and Tim just handed the cashier his $100 bill.

"Oh, for crying out loud," the man behind him said.

"I can't make change for a hundred," the woman said, as if he should know it.

Tim stuffed the bill in his shirt and walked out. He thought of saying, "I didn't want the Moon Pie anyway," but he kept quiet, even to the guy who was behind him.

Then it hit him. The mark on top of the Coke. Someone had probably put something in there that made his stomach writhe like a snake in the cold. They'd planned the whole thing. Even the part where Pete asked to see the tickets, because he hadn't given them back. Four tickets for four guys—only Tim wasn't one of them.

"I hate Christians," Tim muttered.

He sat by a Pepsi machine, the concrete littered with cigarette butts. The sun was hot, and he could still smell Ian's suntan lotion. He looked around and finally found a phone. But who was he kidding? Who could he call?

JAMIE AND HER BROTHER filed into the meeting room while most of the drivers exited. The room served as a chapel on Sunday mornings after the drivers' meeting and was usually about a third full. At just about every race there was some kind of Christian service for drivers, crew members, and their families. Jamie's mom and dad took this seriously and tried to invite everyone they knew.

Jamie scanned the crowd and tried to pick out the visitors from the regulars. One of the guys who led the service last year had preached a message about true believers and ones who just knew about God but didn't do anything about it. The message had offended a few but none more than her.

She tried hard to do what was right, be a good girl, read the Bible, resist temptation, blah, blah, blah. It seemed like the harder she tried to keep the rules, the more rules she broke. She tried to fit in with her youth group, but every time she thought she was getting closer to God she'd look at Cassie Strower and that smile of hers filled with virtue and goodness and all those white teeth and hardly any makeup, and Jamie wanted to puke. She'd never be *anything* like Cassie, and if that was the kind of person God loved, then she didn't have a chance. Maybe, she thought, she could just do her thing and leave God alone and let him do his, and they'd peacefully coexist without hurting each other.

A guy with a guitar sang a song projected on a screen. Most people didn't sing or they sang off-key. Especially the men. Maybe all that noise of the engines made them tone-deaf.

The chaplain got up and introduced the speaker for the day—a pastor from some big church out west who had flown in the night before. Everybody seemed to know him from a book he had written, but Jamie had never heard of him.

He told a funny story about getting picked up at the airport. The driver of the car thought he was picking up a famous NASCAR driver and was disappointed to find out that he was just a pastor.

Everybody laughed, but Jamie wasn't convinced this guy could say anything new.

"I'm not going to use a lot of NASCAR word pictures because, to be honest, I know just enough to
be dangerous. A friend of mine invited me to the
Richard Petty Driving Experience, and after three laps
around the track at 165 mph, I was ready to toss my
cookies."

Laughter.

"I'd have to load up on Dramamine just to watch
a whole race, because even that makes me queasy,
so you don't have anything to worry about from me.
But I do know something about this—" he held up a
Bible—"and I've spent enough time in here to be able
to tell you with all my heart that God wants a relationship with you, and he wants to take you places you've
never been before. He wants to deliver you from lone-
liness and despair. He wants to release you from the
power of things and free you up to be an instrument
he can use for his glory."

The room got quiet as the man paused. Then he
told a story about a king in the Old Testament who had
everything you could imagine—gold and silver and
riches beyond compare. Lots of wives, which made
most of the guys in the room laugh for some reason.
Then the pastor quoted the king, who had written,
"'Everything is meaningless,' says the Teacher, 'completely meaningless!'"

"Those of you who have reached the top know

that it isn't enough. A lot of people have climbed the ladder of success and have found that it was against the wrong building."

More chuckles, but they were subdued. Something was going on in the room, and Jamie couldn't quite figure it out.

"I don't care how much money you win, how many championships, how many fans would follow you around the Denny's parking lot asking for autographs. There is a deep need inside each of us to connect with the one who made us. There's a hole in our soul only one person can fill, and everything else is just meaningless. It's like trying to catch a handful of wind. One minute you think you have it, and the next minute it's gone."

The pastor looked around the room. "There's probably no other group of athletes or athletes' wives and families who understand how fragile life is better than you. And how sweet it is when you give control to the one who has your best interests at heart, who wants to love you with an everlasting love.

"I used to put my hand in my daddy's big old paw and walk with him around our farm. He'd point out the different trees and have me stop to watch a big buck deer step out of a thicket. All the time I thought we were just going for a walk, but he was teaching me. And if you'll slip that hand of yours into your heavenly

Father's hand and walk with him, he'll teach you and love you and guide you in the steps you need to take. But he won't force you. He gives you the choice."

Jamie heard sniffles around the room. Some people reached for tissues and wiped away tears.

The man prayed at the end and asked God to keep everyone safe. He asked God to bless the families and to comfort anyone who was lonely.

Jamie bowed her head and closed her eyes, like she knew she was supposed to. But try as she might, all she could think of was her dream of sitting in this room as a real driver, not a kid listening. Of winning the cup and having enough money to buy whatever she wanted.

Maybe the God stuff was real. Maybe what the pastor said was true—that you could put your hand in the hand of the Almighty and he would show you where you needed to go. But Jamie's fear was that if she did that, if she *really* gave control to someone else, she'd lose her dreams and wind up in some foreign country wearing hand-me-down clothes sent in a box and teaching dirty-faced kids about Jesus, using a flannelgraph board. If she followed God, she feared he would make her give up racing, and she couldn't do that.

As soon as the prayer was over, she slipped out and hurried back to the camper.

"SO YOU SAY THEM old boys just took off without you?" the man said. He had the name Boyd on his work shirt and wore a sweat-stained John Deere hat. His lower lip stuck out, and he spit some brown juice into the dirt by the side of the road. Tim had started walking on a road near the interstate, and the man stopped his motorcycle and walked it alongside him.

"Took my tickets, too," Tim said.

"What are you gonna do when you get there?" Boyd said. "That race was sold out months ago, wasn't it?"

"I know," Tim said. "I just can't see coming this far and not at least trying to get in."

"If that don't beat all," Boyd said, shaking his head. "And you think they spiked your Coca-Cola?" He spat again. "That's down-right criminal is what that is."

The sky had turned a deep blue, and Tim squinted at the sun. "At least it's not raining. Looks like the weather's going to be good. How much farther you think it is?"

Boyd told him, pointing out where he'd need to go under the interstate, then talked about a time when he had been wronged.

Tim tried to concentrate, but all he could think about was Jeff and his buddies. Why would Kimberly introduce him to Jeff if she knew he was a jerk?

The sign for the Daytona International Speedway came up as Tim walked and traffic slowed to a crawl above him.

"Sure am sorry they treated you like that, buddy," Boyd said. He handed Tim $20. "Have lunch on me. And if you see them fellows that dumped you, well, I'd stick something in their tires if I was you."

Tim smiled at the thought. Revenge would be nice. But he'd never find Jeff's SUV in this sea of au-tos. "I thank you for your kindness, stopping like you did," Tim said.

Boyd started his motorcycle and zoomed off.

By the time Tim made his way around the traffic that backed all the way to the interstate and entered the speedway, the race was about to start. In the distance he could see the stands, which were nearly full, and the hundreds of vendors peddling hats, shirts, replica cars, pennants, and just about everything you could imagine. Tim had seen NASCAR officials shut down vendors who were selling unlicensed merchandise. If you weren't selling official gear, you weren't selling.

Guys with hands full of tickets yelled, "Who needs two? I got four right on the infield!"

Tim wondered if Jeff and the others had pocketed a few hundred dollars and headed home or if they were in there.

"What's your cheapest ticket?" Tim said to a man whose hair was the color of shoe polish.

"How many you need, kid?"

"Just one."

"I don't sell individual seats. You gotta buy at least two."

"How much for two?"

Tim's heart fell when he heard the price. It was more than five times what he had.

"Check back as we get closer to race time. I might have a single left."

He tried three other sellers and got a little closer to his range but not enough. He walked out of the parking area, navigating through cars trying to get last-minute parking and driving recklessly. Giving up, he made his way to the Volusia Mall and found the food court. He used the $20 Boyd had given him to buy a pretzel and a bottle of water. He stuffed the change in his pocket and walked to the courtyard, where big-screen TVs carried the race.

I got this close to the race, and I'm watching it on TV, he thought. *How did this happen?*

JAMIE HAD PLEADED with her dad for years to let her be on the pit crew, but there was about as much chance of that happening as him letting her drive the car. It was a highly coordinated, high-skill position that took a lot of practice and preparation. You couldn't just step into that without connections and talent. She could have done PR for her dad, but she was probably a couple of years away from that too. The team liked Jamie, but it was clear she wasn't crew material yet.

She watched from the pits as her parents hugged and kissed. Her dad climbed into the car—he liked to wait until the last moment to get in because he hated being confined—popped on the steering wheel, and got his helmet and HANS device situated.

Soon one of the chaplains came by and prayed with him and patted his helmet. It was a ritual to some people, a good-luck charm to protect them from injury, like wearing their lucky underwear or that pendant their mother gave them. To her dad, it was a lot more. He said it put everything in perspective and gave him a peace he couldn't explain.

After the prayer came the national anthem, which would be followed by the flyover by some military jets. The crowd always responded to them about as much as the moment when a celebrity yelled over the loudspeakers, "Gentlemen, start your engines!" No matter how many races she'd been to, those words and the sound of the engines firing to life always gave her chills.

These moments and the ones that followed separated true fans from the tailgaters or people who'd come for a spectacular crash. Every second of the race was filled with action. Something was going on in every one of the 43 cars. It was a huge chess match, but instead of playing against only one other team, you were playing against 42.

The crew chief for her dad's team, T.J. Kelly, raced over and spoke quickly with her mom as a singer finished "The Star-Spangled Banner." Jamie's mom looked back at her and shook her head. Jamie moved closer.

"Then we gotta pull somebody from the pit crew, and we don't have a hand to spare, Nicole."

The jets flew over and hit the afterburners. The crowd went wild.

Her mother leaned over next to the crew chief's face and yelled, "What does Dale think?"

"It was his idea. Now you've gotta make up your mind fast because we're almost out of time."

"What is it?" Jamie said.

"Scotty's sick," T.J. said. "They think it might be food poisoning. He's pukin' his guts out over the side of the railing. We need somebody to take over the spotter position."

"I can do it," Jamie said to him. She looked at her mother. "Mom, I can do this."

"Jamie, it's dangerous. Your dad—the whole team is affected by this."

"What's the alternative?" Jamie said. "You can't go without a spotter. I've watched this race since I could walk. I know how to talk him through—I've listened to him and Scotty a million times."

"If Scotty recovers, he takes over again," T.J. said.

Jamie nodded.

Her mom sighed. "If it was Dale's idea and that's what he wants, I guess it's the best."

"And you're sure you're okay with that, Jamie?" T.J. said.

"More than okay."

Somebody slapped her on the back. It was Kellen. "Go show 'em what you can do up there."

TIM THOUGHT THE CROWD at the mall courtyard was probably as raucous as the one in the stands. They whooped and yelled each time their favorite drivers were shown. The announcer's audio was turned low, so Tim moved to one of the side speakers so he could hear.

"And we're getting late word that one of the members of Dale Maxwell's team is sick, and they're substituting a new spotter," the man said. "Can you imagine trying to run Daytona with a backup?"

A retired driver responded, "That's like driving one-handed and trying to open a bag of popcorn."

"Wait, we're getting word now that . . . you're not going to believe this."

"Lay it on us."

"Dale Maxwell's new spotter is his

Chapter 18

16-year-old daughter. Can we get a shot of her? . . . Yeah, there she is putting on the headset."

The crowd tittered and gasped around Tim as they showed a close-up of the Maxwell girl. She had a brown ponytail and a pretty face. She tried to get the headset on over the Maxwell hat, but finally she just took the hat off and threw it on the ground. Then the screen switched to her dad's car in a line with all the other racers behind the pace car. Tim's stomach clenched, and he had to turn away.

"Look how young she is," the announcer said. "Are there any restrictions on who you can put up there?"

"I don't think there's an age requirement," the re-tired driver said. "There might be one after this race, though. When the spotter straps that headset on, the driver's putting his life—and the life of every other driver on the track—in that person's hands. I don't like this."

"Well, you can't blame *her*," another announcer said. "She's just filling a hole for that Maxwell team, so if you're going to be upset with somebody, be upset with the crew chief."

"You gotta give her credit for climbing up there," the retired driver said. "Creating controversy with a father-and-daughter team. Not bad for her first race."

JAMIE FINALLY GOT into position and adjusted her headset and both radios. She knew Scotty worked with one radio to talk to the driver and another to listen to NASCAR officials during the race. As soon as she was set, she glanced at the other spotters. They were all staring at her and looked away quickly. Her stomach churned, and she felt like rushing to the bathroom herself, but there was no chance of that now. She was as locked and loaded as a policeman's handgun at a bank robbery.

She'd listened to chatter on the radio since she was young, and she knew all the words, all the familiar phrases. But nothing had prepared her for this.

"How you feeling up there, Jamie?" her dad said.

"New experience," she said. "I finally get to tell *you* how to drive."

Chapter 19

"I didn't think of that." Her dad laughed.

"Pace car's falling off," the crew chief said. "You two ready to rock 'n roll?"

"Ready," Jamie said.

"Bring it on," her dad said.

Jamie took a deep breath and let it out. Then she keyed the mic. "All right, here we go. Flag coming out. Green, green, green."

The other spotters said something similar to their drivers as the cars screamed past the start line. Jamie felt like a billion butterflies had camped in her stomach overnight, and they were all stretching and flying at the same time.

More than 160,000 fans cheered, the sound deafening, but Jamie kept her eye on the #14 Maxwell car. At 2.5 miles around the track, her dad would pass her again in less than a minute.

Jamie saw a car in turn two swerve near her father's car. "Watch it. . . . Stay up, stay up. The #46 car had a little wobble there in the turn."

"I got it," her dad said.

"You're doing good, Jamie," T.J. said. "Just relax and get a feel for what's going on."

"We're bunching up pretty good down here," her dad said. "I'm gonna ride the train for a lap or two. You relax, little girl."

On the third lap, Jamie keyed the mic. "I've seen two spots where you've been clear low, Dad."

"Okay. Let me know if you think I can make it."

They were 20 laps into the race when a clear spot opened. Jamie hesitated, and the moment was lost.

Two laps later she saw another opening and keyed her mic. "Clear low," Jamie said as calmly as she could. "Go."

The Maxwell car veered low into the turn, passed the #22 car, and took position in front of him. Jamie was amazed at how three words changed their position so quickly. It gave her a feeling of power, just like racing, only hers were the eyes on the roof and not the hands turning the wheel.

A plume of smoke rose, and the crowd gasped.

"Trouble in turn two, Dad. Stay low, low, low." Her heart pounded as her dad shot past a car with smoke billowing from its rear. "Yellow flag. Yellow flag."

Someone tapped her on the shoulder. It was Scotty, his face as pale as one of her mom's white sheets.

"You look awful," she said.

"What's wrong with me?" her dad said on the radio.

She'd pushed the mic button by mistake. "Sorry, Dad. Scotty's here. Looks like I'm handing you off to him."

"All right. Great job, Jamie."

Spotter after spotter patted her on the back as she moved toward the stairs, but she couldn't bear to go down them. Something told her to stay right where she was.

The TV broadcast replayed some of her communication with her dad.

"Still have the same opinion?" the announcer said.

The commentator laughed. "Boy, I'll tell you what—that girl knows what she's doing up there. Just as calm and cool as they come."

Jamie blushed and smiled, wondering if Kellen and her mom had seen the replay.

It was on lap 150 that the big problem happened. Not a crash into the wall or a nudge that led to a spin-out. Scotty keeled over and smacked the back of his head. Another spotter helped him up, and Jamie was there, ripping the headset off. Scotty was up—wobbly, but up.

"Probably needs fluids," T.J. said to Jamie when she explained what had happened. "Tell him to get downstairs and stay there. You're taking us the rest of the way, you hear?"

Jamie knew that fans were waiting for the big one. Daytona and Talladega were known as two of the most dangerous races because of the speeds on the straightaway. They had gone 175 laps without a serious accident, and the tension was mounting. Her dad was in the middle of a pack, three across, when she noticed the car behind him.

"Number 13 right behind you, Dad. Getting closer."

"He just bumped me," her dad said.

"Tell Devalon's spotter to back off!" the crew chief yelled.

Jamie turned and saw the black-clad #13 spotter at the far end. No way was she going to run down there. "Hey, 13!" she screamed.

The thin man held up a hand. "Tell Dale he's sorry."

She keyed the mic. "You're not going to believe this, but the Devalon guy just said sorry."

"You're right. I don't believe it."

"Clear, clear, all clear behind that 79 car," Jamie said three laps later.

Her dad followed her direction and made the move. "Now I know why," he said. "Lots of water spitting out—or maybe coolant. It's all over the—"

The crowd gasped, and Jamie couldn't speak as her dad fishtailed out of the turn, bumped from behind by #13.

"Hang on to it, Dale!" the crew chief said.

All she could do was watch in horror as the

Maxwell car shifted right and took out #44 and #12, pushing them into the wall. Then the three cars spun out, careening to the bottom of the track and right in the path of several cars behind. Unscathed, #13 darted left and avoided them.

The cars behind them weren't so lucky. In all, 12 cars crashed and were taken out of the race. Jamie's dad's was one of them.

"Yellow flag," she said, scowling at the Devalon spotter.

The man just chuckled and shook his head.

NEAR THE END OF THE race, Tim
wandered toward the track, but security was still tight. There was no slip-
ping through some hole in the fence
here. The roar of the crowd signaled the
end of the race. For once, he didn't care
who won.

He sat by an underpass as the exo-
dus began. Getting 165,000 people out
of the stands, into their cars, and back
on the road would take a while, but
Daytona was known as one of the better cup races to exit.

He knew what was going on inside—the packing and loading and
cleanup. Crashed cars were getting cut
up to fit in the hauler. The winner's car
was being taken apart piece by piece
and inspected. He didn't envy the
crews inside, but it was one of those
mindless jobs he was always good at.

He could kick into high gear and pack with the best of them.

When darkness fell and most of the cars were gone from the parking area, he walked to the back entrance, where he could see the trucks getting ready to pull out. A security officer had his eye on him, so Tim stayed back, waiting.

When he saw the trademark hat of Charlie Hale, he started waving and jumping like crazy. The light was fading, so he sprinted up the access road and got in the headlights. The truck honked, like he was just some fan who wanted attention, but Tim didn't give up. He ran beside the road on the gravel, waving his hat.

"Get out of the way, kid!" Charlie yelled in his familiar strangled voice.

"Charlie, it's me! Tim Carhardt!"

At that, Charlie's beagle, Chester, barked, and the truck pulled to the side of the road.

Tim dodged a passing truck and ran around to the passenger side.

The door was open and Charlie waved. "What're you waiting for? Climb in!"

The truck still had that old dog smell. Charlie moved a bunch of stuff to the back in order for Tim to get in, and soon they were on the road.

"You see the race?" Charlie said.

"No, there was a mix-up. It's a long story. Who won?"

Charlie told him. It wasn't a surprise. Tim asked how his new employer had done and how he liked driving for him. Charlie said he was glad to have a ride.

The radio was tuned to a country station, and the CB crackled with the voices of big rig drivers. "You picking up hitchhikers now, Charlie?" one of them said on the radio.

"I got Timmy Carhardt in the cab with me," Charlie said, clicking the mic.

The radio was dead for a minute.

"Tell Tim we said hello," the driver replied. About half a dozen of them echoed his words or double clicked their mics.

"How'd you get down here?" Charlie said.

"I not only lost my tickets, but I lost my ride back to Tallahassee. I assume you guys are headed straight back to Charlotte."

"That's right. I'd love to take you over there, but I got a deadline."

"I understand. Do you think you could just let me off near Jacksonville? I could call my cousin from there."

Charlie thought awhile, which meant there were a few minutes of just the country music and the crackle of the CB. Finally, looking straight at the road, he said, "We miss your dad out here. It's not the same without him."

"Yeah. Same here."

"You getting along all right?"

"I'm in school now, making lots of friends." He didn't know why he lied. Maybe he wanted Charlie to think everything was okay with him. "And the people I'm staying with are good to me."

"That's good. I always wondered where you went. Must have been a tough last few months."

The sound of the road and the squawk of the CB and the radio brought everything back. It was like coming home again.

"Charlie, what do you think the chances would be of me coming back and riding with a team again? I'd pull my weight. Help with anything."

"I thought you said you had it good in this new situation."

"Yeah, I do, but . . ."

"You miss Chester, don't you?"

They both laughed, and Tim scratched the dog's head. "Yeah, there's nobody like old Chester. It's a pretty far-fetched idea, I know. Maybe after I finish school, huh?"

"Yeah, that's a good idea. Finish school and see if you still want to get back out here."

When they neared Jacksonville, Charlie put out a call on his CB to a family he knew that was headed west from there. The father turned out to be a man Charlie had worked with years before in Andalusia, Alabama.

"We have an extra seat, no problem," the man said when they met at a gas station. "Hope you don't mind riding with some snoring kids in the back."

"Don't mind at all," Tim said.

Tim thanked Charlie and gave Chester a good-bye pat on the head. Charlie tried to say something, but he finally just lightly punched Tim on the shoulder and ambled off to his truck.

They were a few miles down the road when the dad looked in the rearview mirror and asked Tim where he lived and how he'd liked the race. Most of the others in the car were asleep.

In Tallahassee, Tim asked the man to drop him at a nearby convenience store. He offered to pay the man for his trouble, but he wouldn't take anything.

"See you, Tim," the mother said from the front, shifting in her seat for a better position.

The man stepped out of the car. "I know all about what happened to you. Last year at Talladega, right?"

"Yeah, that was my dad."

The man put a hand on Tim's shoulder. "I want

you to know how sorry we are. Afterward I read a story in the paper that mentioned you. Our family has been praying for you ever since."

"I appreciate that, sir," Tim said. "I wish I'd have met you folks before I headed to Daytona."

The man handed him a business card with his phone number on it. "Anything you need, call me." He bit his lip. "Do you know the Lord, son?"

Tim nodded. "Oh yeah." He said it because he knew that's what the man wanted to hear. But the truth was, Tim wanted to finish his sentence with *and I don't want anything to do with him.*

"You'll be okay from here?" the man said.

"Yeah, my place is just back there. I thank you for your kindness."

Tim walked the rest of the way home, past a few barking dogs. A raccoon was in a garbage can, its tail twitching. It looked right at Tim, then went back to the half-eaten bag of microwave popcorn.

The front door was locked, and Tim didn't have a key. He jimmied his window open and crawled through, landing on his bed. He lay there a few minutes, listening for anyone stirring in the rest of the trailer. Fully clothed, his backpack still slung around his arm, Tim fell asleep and didn't wake up until he was late for school the next day.

JAMIE TRIED TO SLEEP, stretched out in the middle seat of the family's Suburban, but she couldn't get the sight of her dad's wrecked car out of her head. Or the sight of Butch Devalon standing by his car at the end of the race, pumping his fists, his crew whooping around him and shaking champagne bottles all over. The Devalons were probably already home. Like a lot of teams, they had flown their jet to Daytona.

She'd seen the replay of the wreck a few times in the camper and cringed when one of the announcers asked Devalon to explain what happened. "Well, that was unfortunate. I got a little excited in the middle of the pack and kind of bumped Dale. I was lucky to get out of there without damage to the car, and we had us a good one today. Took us all the way to the finish line."

"What's it feel like to be leader in points after the first race of the season?" the announcer said.

"Feels real good to get a win. A win is good any-time of the year but especially to start the season. I'm happy as a clam. Of course, it's a long season, so we'll just have to see what happens."

Burrowing around Jamie's brain was the conversa-tion she'd had with Butch Devalon. Was he setting her up, or did the Devalon team really want to sign her? She couldn't talk with her dad about it and wouldn't, unless Kellen opened his big mouth.

"Hey, Dad," Jamie whispered. He turned down MRN on the radio, and Jamie looked at her mother, fast asleep beside him, her face illuminated by the dashboard lights. "Did Scotty tell you what he ate that made him so sick?"

Scotty had been taken to a nearby hospital and had to stay overnight. The doctors said he needed flu-ids, and they wanted to watch him.

Her dad chuckled. "You know Scotty. He'll eat al-most anything that isn't on the move. He made the rounds of the different haulers. It's hard to tell what it was, but I can tell you this: as sick as he got, he'll stick with our food from now on."

Jamie's mind swirled with everything from Chad to her dad's interview after the race.

Her dad's familiar voice came on the radio, answering a question from a reporter. "Well, it's just one of those things that happens. The car was running well, and I felt like we had a good chance, but you have to take the good with the bad. Everything happens for a reason, and we've got a long season ahead."

She looked at her dad and could tell from his face, even if no one else could, that he was mad.

"How'd you feel up there with the spotters?" her dad whispered.

"Good, I guess. I hate that I couldn't get you out of that mess."

"You did great," he said. "I was real comfortable with you watching my back. Maybe you were the one who gave Scotty the bad food."

Jamie laughed.

"Any more thoughts about selling your cars?"

"Yeah. This is something I really want to do, Dad. I know you're against it. . . ."

He stretched and put his arm on the seat back and patted her arm. "I've been thinking about it a lot. I want to give you the go-ahead. I want to work with you so you can reach your dream. I just have this gut feeling that it's not the right time. And if I was to give in on this when I feel so strongly, it wouldn't be right." She leaned back, and he looked in the rearview mirror. "Let's keep talking. Gonna be a hairy few days, trying to get the car in shape for California, but we can hash this out. There's nobody who's more on your team than me."

Jamie closed her eyes. Butch Devalon's face flashed through her mind. She leaned forward and touched his shoulder. "Thanks for trusting me with the spotter's job. Maybe you can return the favor someday."

"You got it, kid."

Jamie looked at her mom. Did she sleep with a smile, or was that there because she'd heard every word?

TIM WALKED TO Community Church, a sprawling building with a parking lot as big as a shopping mall's. There were flags around one building with windows that ran from the ground all the way to the roof. He spotted the red SUV toward the front of the lot. He glanced at the building to make sure no one was watching. The place looked deserted.

He pulled out his pocketknife and went to work, shoving the blade into the sidewalls. He thought about smashing the windshield, but that felt a little like overkill.

The tires were flat within a couple of minutes, and he walked away slowly, like he'd just been out for a stroll. Headlights shone in the distance, and two vans pulled in. He froze, a deer in the headlights. More like a deer holding

Chapter 22
Caught

a sharp knife in the headlights. He quickly closed the knife and shoved it in his pocket.

The van stopped near him, but he kept walking. A door opened on the other side, closed, and the van sped away. He kept his head down, his hat pulled low.

"Tim?" someone shouted. A girl's voice.

He turned to see Kimberly heading toward him.

"Did you just get here? We've been over at the soup kitchen. We do that once a month. You want to come in? We have a short meeting inside before the night's over."

"I gotta get home."

"Oh, how'd Daytona go? I heard it was a good race."

"Yeah, exciting."

"Everything work out with Jeff?"

"Sort of. He here tonight?"

"No, he only shows up when there's food or bowling. Actually, I felt kind of bad suggesting him because he's not one of our strongest guys, if you know what I mean. I don't even know that he's a believer, but I do know he's a big race fan."

"Wait," Tim said, his heart racing. "He's not here tonight? Isn't that his car?"

"I don't think so. He drives a ratty old thing that's falling apart. I can get you his phone number, if you'd like."

///////

Two days later a police officer showed up at the trailer park and asked to talk to Tim. Tyson wasn't home from work, and Vera was more than a little agitated to see a badge at their door. What would the neighbors think? Tim was sure that was going through her mind.

"Were you over at the Community Church a couple of nights ago?" the officer said. He was a stern-faced guy with a military haircut.

Tim knew Kimberly had seen him, so he couldn't lie. "Yeah, I was there. Just cutting through the parking lot."

"Where were you going?"

"On my way home."

"You know anything about four slashed tires?"

Tim hesitated.

"Why don't you come with me."

Tyson pulled in as they were driving away. Tim thought about waving at him from the back of the squad car, but he didn't.

Instead of taking him to the police station and throwing him in jail, which is what Tim thought would happen, the cop drove to the church and escorted Tim to the front desk, where a woman dialed a number. She hung up and told them they could go in. They walked upstairs to an office area. The cop seemed to know where he was going.

"They keep a surveillance camera going 24-7," the officer said. "They caught you in the act, but we didn't know who you were until we found the girl you were talking to."

Great, Tim thought. *Ratted out by Miss Christian Teen America.*

The pastor met them at his office door and shook hands with the officer. He stood in a long room with lots of books on mahogany shelves.

Tim couldn't help but notice the old coins in a glass case. He'd seen ones from the 1800s, but these looked even older.

"Thanks for helping with this," the pastor said to the officer, then turned to Tim. "He's a member of our congregation here. He agreed to help us work this out."

"I'll be downstairs," the officer said.

"Have a seat, Tim." The pastor offered him one of the overstuffed chairs by his desk, then sat facing him. "You want to tell me why, of all the cars in the parking lot, you chose mine? Have I done something to upset you?"

"I'm sorry about your car," Tim said. "It was a mistake."

The man's brow was furrowed, and Tim imagined

it was the way he looked when he preached about hell. But there was something about his eyes that made Tim want to tell him the truth. So he did. The whole story of meeting Jeff and getting stiffed on the way to Daytona just spilled out.

The man listened, his hands together, index fingers resting on his lower lip. "Sounds like a bad experience," he said when Tim finished. "Why didn't you smash the windshield?"

"I thought about it."

The man smiled. "So what do you think I ought to do?"

Tim thought a moment. "If I paid you back for the tires, would you call it square?"

He nodded. "I think that would work. Do you have a job?"

"Not yet." He reached in his pocket. "But I got $100. That's a good start—don't you think?"

The man dipped his head in thought. "Tell you what. Keep that until I find out exactly how much it's going to cost. You seem like a responsible young man. Maybe you just had a lapse in judgment. You don't have a police record." He grabbed a piece of paper from his desk. "We have a janitorial position that hasn't been filled. It's three nights and weekends. You'd clean up after the kids' meetings and church services. Not very glamorous but it pays. You interested?"

After what had happened with Jeff, Tim didn't want anything to do with any church on the face of the planet. But this guy seemed evenhanded, and Tim needed the money to pay him back for his tires. "How much?"

The pastor told him the hourly rate. It sounded more than fair. Probably more than Tyson made an hour.

"Okay, I'll do it. Just until I get your tires paid off."

JAMIE'S AD FOR MAXIE went in the paper the next week. She cleaned and polished both cars until they shone. She'd scraped Maxie against a concrete pole in the school parking lot, and she tried to paint it herself but couldn't match the color. Only two people came to look that week, and one made an offer. It was half of what the car was worth.

Jamie's dad raced at the California Speedway the next weekend, and people from their church gathered to watch at the house. It was a tradition that the people in her mom and dad's Bible study got together and prayed before the races in the spring and fall, when the family didn't travel with him.

Jamie was as polite as she could be, but when she saw Vanessa Moran, she couldn't believe it.

"Jamie, you know Vanessa from church, don't you?" her mom said.

"Yeah," she said, not impolite but not necessarily inviting either. As soon as she could, she excused herself and retreated to the garage. She flipped on the black-and-white TV on the workbench and changed Maxie's oil.

"So this is what you do in your spare time?" Vanessa said, venturing into the garage like it was some foreign country. When Jamie held out her oil-stained hands, the girl made a face.

"What did you think they ran on, sugar and spice?" Jamie said.

"You don't have to get surly about it. How's your dad doing?"

Jamie turned up the volume. "He's having wedge problems, and he cut a tire in a spinout. Just got the blue flag."

Vanessa squinted at the tiny screen. "How can you tell all that? I thought they just went around and around until somebody won."

Jamie wiped her hands on a rag and pushed hair from her face. "There's a lot of teamwork and strategy to racing." She almost started to explain, but she figured it would be wasted on Vanessa.

"No, go on. Tell me more. Maybe I can teach my dad. All he knows is how much money everybody makes. What's the blue flag?"

"They have different colored flags to communicate to drivers. Green means go, of course. The checkered flag . . . well, you have to know what the checkered flag means."

"They're supposed to stop and play checkers? No, I know—it's the one the winner gets. But I've never seen a blue flag."

"It's got a yellow stripe on it. If you get that, you're supposed to let the lead cars pass you."

"Kind of like a yield sign."

"You got it."

"That can't be good."

"Like I said, he's had his problems. But the race is 500 miles, so he's got time to catch up." Jamie looked at the screen again. "These guys in the lead are on the same team. They're going to work together to finish as high as they can."

"You mean they help each other out?"

Jamie nodded. "You get points for leading the most laps, for winning a race, and other stuff. The driver with the most points at the end of the year wins the cup. They also have team winners. Now the guy in third, he's drafting them both to go faster, and at some point he'll try to pass—"

"Why are they all in a line like that?"

"Cuts down the wind resistance." She used her hands to explain. "When the cars go 180 or 190 in the straightaway, like at Daytona or Talladega, the wind slows them down. But if a car pulls right up behind them, the wind is displaced—it just goes over the cars easier and makes them go faster. Add another car or two, and it makes the whole group move faster. The California Speedway isn't as long, so you don't get those speeds. But if you try to pull out and pass from that pack, you can find yourself all the way at the back."

"How do they know when they can pass?"

"That's where the spotter comes in. The drivers have radios to communicate with people on the roof of the grandstand. They tell them when they're clear to pass."

"Wait, they don't look in their mirrors? That would be freaky just to take somebody's word for it."

"That's why you basically trust your spotter with your life. Make a mistake there and you wipe out a lot of people's chances to win."

Vanessa glanced at the TV. "And this is what you do in your spare time? Race that car?"

"Not Maxie. I race that one over there."

"Looks kind of old."

"It's a Legend car. It's supposed to look like that. But don't let looks fool you. I can go fast."

"You have to wear those big coverall thingies?"

"It's called a fire-retardant suit. Yeah, I wear that along with a full-face helmet, gloves, neck brace. The whole deal."

"Ever wreck?"

"A couple of times."

"What happened?"

"Went to the hospital. The first one gave me whip-lash the size of Montana. In the second one I jammed my knee into the steering column. Had a bone contusion and pulled a muscle. Oh, and a concussion."

"Just a little thing like that."

"Yeah. Once you get into a bad wreck, you know whether you really want to race or not. They don't bother me that much." Jamie could tell Vanessa was on information overload, so she screwed the oil filter on and checked for leaks.

When she stood up, Vanessa was focused on the screen. "What's all that white smoke coming out of your dad's car?"

"Great," Jamie muttered. "That's just what he needed."

The mood in the house was somber when Jamie went back inside. Jamie's mom frowned, and Kellen was lying in front of the TV, his knuckles on both cheeks, staring at the screen. "He drove straight to the garage." He sighed.

The yellow flag was out, and a camera caught one of the main sponsors for the Maxwell car.

"That look says it all," the announcer said. "There

are rumblings of a sponsor shake-up in the Maxwell camp—"

"A shake*out* you mean," a commentator said. "Unless there's a major turnaround, we could be seeing some big changes."

Jamie's mom turned down the sound, and the room got really quiet.

"It's only one race," Vanessa said. "Why are they making such a big deal?"

No one said a word.

"Well, Nicole," Mrs. Moran said, "have you heard any more about your addition?"

Jamie caught her mom's gaze, and there seemed to be a bit of fear mixed with nerves. "No, uh, it's sort of on hold." She glanced at Jamie. "But thanks for asking."

Jamie didn't know exactly what was up, but those looks meant her mom was hiding something. And Jamie was determined to find out what it was.

TIM WATCHED ABOUT HALF the California race until it was time to go to work. He was supposed to clean up after a middle school meeting in one of the upstairs rooms. When he got there, it was still going, and he kicked himself for not staying at home longer and catching more of the race.

He spotted a TV in the church kitchen. A couple flips of the channels and he found the California Speedway—a bit grainy, sure, but he could still see it.

With 15 laps to go, the #13 Devalon car was in third, a sign that the Demon of Daytona was back. With his first-place finish there, he was in a good spot to challenge the perennial leaders for the Chase. Of course, any lead this early in the season was suspect, but if the guy kept driving like this, he'd be able to buy several more RVs.

Tim couldn't help standing close to the TV, feeling the excitement of the last laps and the jockeying for position. A nudge here. A push there. This was always the most tense moment of any race—and the most fun to watch.

The door opened, and one of the pastors stuck his head in. "The middle schoolers are finished." He glanced at his watch. "We've got senior high in the same room in less than an hour, and there's Silly String everywhere."

"I'm on it," Tim said.

He took one last look—only nine laps to go—then switched off the TV and locked the door. He grabbed his stuff and headed to the room, which was worse than he imagined. There wasn't just Silly String everywhere; there was Silly String mixed with ground-in pizza and soda.

Tim worked as fast as he could, mopping the tile first, then cleaning the carpet. He imagined he was changing tires on a pit crew. He wanted the pastor and the others at the church to like his work, but his real reason for going so fast was that he wanted to be finished before the high schoolers got there.

The room was looking respectable when the first few kids hit the door. Loners like him. A girl with long curly hair, her nose stuck in a book. A fat kid who crossed his arms over his chest and sat in the back.

He had everything ready and was wheeling the huge, gray trash can into the hall when a gaggle of high schoolers echoed through the hall. He pulled his hat low and went out the side door. He thought he heard Kimberly's voice, and he was glad he didn't have to face her.

After the noise died, Tim wheeled the squeaky trash can and the bucket and mop toward the service elevator in the back. He had just entered the hall when he heard footsteps.

"That's him," someone whispered.

"You sure?" another said. "He's punier than you described."

"Check out his pants. Low budget all the way."

Though he knew he ought to keep going, Tim stopped in the middle of the hall. He recognized one voice.

"Hey, Tim," Jeff said. "Not very good etiquette dumping your friends on the highway like that. Get it? *Dumping?*"

Tim turned. Jeff stood with two guys—neither of them from the car. They looked like they were football team material. Big shoulders. Mops of hair hung over their eyes. Tim tried to think of something snappy to say to put Jeff in his place, but all he could do was stare.

"I hear you like a cold Coke," one of the hulks

said, smiling. The guy had perfect white teeth, and Tim wondered how much his parents had paid for the dental work.

"He likes 'em cold and full of liquid Ex-Lax," Jeff laughed. "Hey, you get the room clean in there? Or did you just eat all the leftovers? If I find any crumbs, I'll fix a plate for you."

"What a loser," the other hulk said.

"Yeah, if I was his dad, I'd have died too." Jeff pushed Tim as he passed the trash.

Jeff didn't see the mop coming, and Tim scored a direct hit to the side of the guy's face. He fell back and gasped as the wet mop stuck to his head.

Tim cursed. "You owe me for those tickets!"

Jeff wiped wet pizza bits from his face and shirt, but when he tried to stand, Tim hit him in the mouth again, shoving him back. The other two were up and on Tim in a flash, wrestling him to the ground, then dragging him toward the stairwell.

"Hey, stop it!" Kimberly shouted. "Let go of him!"

"Get back in the room," Jeff yelled, pulling his shirt up and wiping his face. "This is none of your business."

Tim kicked and thrashed as the three pulled him to the fire door. He managed to get a look at the hall before the doors closed. Kimberly was running the other way, toward the pastor's office.

AS USUAL, WHEN JAMIE got upset, she didn't care that there were people from church around. She didn't care if no one was there or if the room was as full as a shopping mall at Christmas. She let her questions fly. "Why do I have to find out stuff about our family from somebody I don't even know? Do you know how that makes me feel?"

Her mother pulled her into the kitchen as the volume on the TV went back up. "Keep your voice down."

"So your church friends won't hear us fighting? So they'll think we're the perfect family?"

"No. They know we're not perfect."

"Yeah, you've probably told them all about how bad I am."

"Jamie, I don't care what they think of me. I don't want you making a fool of yourself. These are nice people who care about us. They know we have struggles just like they do. Now sit down."

Jamie crossed her arms and kept standing, her back against the wall, knee out, foot propped halfway up the wall. "What was Mrs. Moran talking about? What 'addition' are we adding? Are you and Dad expanding the house?"

"No, nothing like that. We've been talking about a change. We would have told you, but—"

"Mom, what's going on?"

She ran a hand across the tablecloth. "You know I can't have any more children."

"Yeah, I know." Jamie's voice softened. "And you want to adopt some Chinese-Russian baby."

Her mom smiled. "No. Overseas adoption was our first choice because there are so many kids out there who need a home."

"Was?"

"Well, it's still a dream. There are a lot of costs we can't swing right now, but something else has come up. We were going to tell you and Kellen soon. . . ."

"Why did I have to hear it from Mrs. Moran?"

"We asked the people in our Bible study to pray with us about this decision. It's not an easy choice because it's going to change things around here. But this is something your dad feels really strongly about."

"The classes you've been taking—is that connected with this?"

Her mom nodded. "We have to take classes to qualify—"

"Mom, just tell me."

"Honey, let's talk after everyone leaves."

TIM STRUGGLED AT THE top of the stairs. His dad had never taught him to fight. He didn't have to. Tim could handle kids a lot bigger than him just by using his arms and legs. He wasn't muscular, but he was wiry and quick. Once, when he was emptying some trash behind a truck stop, a couple of guys had jumped him. There were glass bottles in both trash bags, and when he swung them, they clinked against his attackers' heads. He'd tossed the bags into the Dumpster and backed away as they stumbled in the dark.

Now one of Jeff's buddies held Tim's arms. He tightened his stomach and took several punches to the gut. Jeff moved left, cocking his arm and aiming for Tim's face. Tim lifted his feet and kicked Jeff's chest. Jeff lost his balance and tumbled backward, grabbing the railing. He scraped his forehead against the blocks, and blood trickled from the wound.

"You're gonna wish you hadn't done that," Jeff growled, scampering back up the steps.

"You oughta wish you hadn't stolen my tickets," Tim said.

"Hold him!" Jeff yelled.

The stairwell door burst open, and one of the pastors ran through, Kimberly right behind him.

"Let him go!" the man said.

The two dropped Tim, and he fell hard to the floor.

"He started it," Jeff hollered, holding out his shirt. "He attacked me with a mop, and we were just defending ourselves."

"Three against one?" Kimberly said. "You gotta be kidding me."

The pastor told Jeff and his friends to go back to the senior high room.

"I don't want any part of this church," Jeff scoffed. "You hire thugs and turn them into janitors. You ought to control them."

"Just settle down," the pastor said.

"No. My dad knows a good lawyer. We could sue this church for being attacked by one of your employees."

Kimberly helped Tim up as the three headed down the stairs and out the side entrance.

The senior pastor opened the stairwell door and stared at Tim. "You okay?"

"Little more excitement than I wanted," Tim said, holding his stomach. "I'll be all right."

The senior pastor closed the door to his office and sat across from Tim. Services were over, and the church was basically empty. The look on the man's face gave him away.

"You don't have to say it," Tim said. "I know what's gonna happen."

"You've done a good job in the short time you've been here, Tim. You're a hard worker, and I'm sure if your dad were here, he'd say he was proud of you."

"If my dad were here, I'd never be caught dead here. No offense."

"None taken. If I could roll back the clock and bring your dad back, I'd do it in a second."

"But . . . ," Tim said.

"Yes. But. I wanted to help you as much as I could and stuck my neck out to get you this job. Several on the elder board were here tonight, and they heard what happened. I'm afraid we're going to have to let you go."

"I understand." He pulled out the $100 bill and put it on the pastor's desk. "I'll still pay you the rest."

The pastor waved a hand. "You keep this. As far as I'm concerned, we're square."

"I'm real sorry about your tires."

"I hope you won't let this whole thing cloud your thoughts about God. He cares more for you than you know. I'd like to talk with you about that sometime."

Tim rose, his ribs sore and his face swollen. "I'm sure you mean well, but I don't think God wants much to do with me."

The man's eyes watered. "Tim, I believe everybody is put on earth for a purpose. God made you. He has a destiny for you. I can tell it just by spending a little time with you."

Tim shoved the $100 into his pocket. "You don't know me. If I could've thrown those guys down the stairs, I'd have done it. So don't tell me how much God loves me or has a purpose for me. He doesn't care about me, and I don't care about him."

Tim left the office, the pastor in his chair, staring at the floor.

Kimberly waited for him in the hallway. She wrung her hands. "This is all my fault. I was the one who introduced you to Jeff."

"You didn't know he was a skunk. I should have realized it when I got in his car."

She followed like a puppy to the janitor's closet

as Tim put away his tools. "I hope you won't let this make you not want to come to church."

Tim couldn't hide a grin. "No, I can't think of anything I'd rather do than praise the Lord by getting beat up. It's a real worshipful experience."

IT TOOK AN HOUR for the people to leave the Maxwell house after the race was over. Jamie stayed in her room until the last car left. Everybody seemed really sad at the outcome of the race, but she could hear them encouraging her mom as they walked to their cars.

When Jamie's dad called, she got on the phone and listened from upstairs. He was staying in California and heading with the crew to Las Vegas for the next race—a place he hated, but it was too expensive to travel back and forth.

A few minutes later her mom yelled for Kellen to pick up.

"I'm sorry you heard about this from somebody else," her dad said.

"You've always said we're a team," Jamie said. "Why wouldn't you let us in on your plan?"

Chapter 27

"What plan?" Kellen said. "What are you guys talking about?"

Her dad cleared his throat. "There's a kid down in Florida whose father died at Talladega."

"The Carhardt guy?" Kellen said.

"Exactly. We've talked to his social worker and found out that he's not in a really good place. He's 15, so it's not going to be long before he can be out on his own, but over the last few weeks, your mother and I have felt like God's calling us to give him a home."

"Wow, a big brother," Kellen said. "Would he change his name to Maxwell?"

"We don't even know if he'll want to live here," Mom said. "But we want to give it a shot."

"This whole thing is contingent on you two, though," Dad said.

"What's *contingent* mean?" Kellen said.

"It means you should be quiet," Jamie said.

"You guys can vote against it if you don't like it. We're not going to push this on you unless you agree. You're as much a part of the decision making as we are."

Jamie fumed. "Okay, so you go through all these classes and then say it's up to us?"

"Jamie—"

"No, you're saying God is telling you to do this, but we can veto it. That's great. God's on your side, and we're on the other."

"I didn't mean it like that," her dad said. "I'm just trying to shoot straight."

"I think it's a great idea," Kellen said. "He can help me with my homework. And he's probably better at math than Jamie too."

Nobody laughed.

"What do you think, Jamie?" her mom said.

Jamie thought about the Devalon team. Her car. Her dreams. Did her parents care more about this guy in Florida they didn't even know than about her?

"Fine," she said, then hung up.

TIM DIDN'T TELL TYSON or Vera about what had happened at the church or with Jeff. He hoped they'd never find out. When he saw Lisa's car outside their trailer, his heart sank. He liked the woman, but every time she came around it seemed like trouble followed.

He walked near the front window to see if he could overhear any of the conversation inside, but the hum of the air conditioner drowned everything out.

He moved past a window and heard Vera say, "Here he is now." She opened the door and told him to come in. "What are you doing hanging around out here?"

"Thought I lived here."

"Not for long," Vera said.

Tim walked inside. Lisa looked out of place with this family, like a nice piece of furniture sitting next to a trash can on the curb.

Chapter 28

She smiled at him and asked him to sit. "How'd you like Daytona?" she said. "Everything go okay?"

Tim stole a glance at Tyson and his wife. "There were a couple of glitches with that. But thanks for the tickets."

"Miss Lisa has some news for you, Tim," Vera said with a surprisingly sweet tone.

"We've been contacted by someone who's asked if you'd like to come live with them," Lisa said.

"They volunteered?"

Lisa nodded. "The parents know about you and talked with their two kids, and everybody agreed they'd like to have you move to North Carolina."

"But they're not family," Tyson said. "Blood's always thicker. You're our relative, and we want you here."

"The father is a driver," Lisa continued, ignoring Tyson.

"What's he drive? Truck series?"

Lisa's eyes widened, and her face got tight, as if she'd forgotten to study for an important test. "I'm not sure. I know he was on TV last weekend. He drives the #14 car."

Tim's jaw stiffened. "Maxwell?"

"You know him! That's awesome. He and his wife sound really nice. They've already qualified as a foster family and—"

"Not interested," Tim said. He grabbed his back-pack and headed outside.

"Tim, why not?"

"Leave the boy alone," Tyson said. "He's made his decision."

Lisa followed Tim outside and caught up with him at the little park near the edge of the forest. "Hey, don't run away like that. I'm not the enemy here. I'm *for* you. What's going on?"

"I don't want to move to North Carolina."

"You don't have to do anything, but I've got to think their place would be a lot better than here. Help me understand."

"I'm not living anywhere close to that guy."

"What's the problem with Dale Maxwell?"

Tim set his jaw and finally looked at Lisa. "I'll tell you what's wrong. He's the guy who ran into my dad. He's the one who killed him."

JAMIE'S DAD FARED A LITTLE better in the next race in Las Vegas, finishing 23rd. She was just glad he finished rather than blowing an engine or crashing. In the next three weeks in Atlanta and then the short tracks of Bristol and Martinsville, he managed to finish in the top 20, but there were still rumblings from the main sponsor, and since money fueled the teams and cars as much as the gas, home was tense. Dallas was a disaster. He blew out a tire to some track debris and lost second gear heading out of the pits. By the end of the race he'd lost third gear as well and was penalized for going too fast in the pit area.

Jamie's car went unsold, and she pulled out of several races. She heard through some friends that Chad hadn't raced yet but was burning up the local track with practice time.

Chapter 29
More Trouble

A flurry of phone calls had come from a woman in Florida. Jamie had been on her way to her job at the car-parts store when she called, asking for her mom. Jamie said she'd take a message.

"Are you Jamie?" the woman said.

"Yeah."

"Just tell her Lisa called from Tallahassee."

"Are you the one trying to get a home for the Carhardt guy?"

"That's me. But I'm not having much success. How are things in your world?"

There was something about the woman's voice that seemed inviting. Like she was someone Jamie could trust. "Pretty good. Looks like I might get my car sold."

"You have your own car?"

Jamie told her about Maxie and all she'd done to it.

"Sounds like a member of the family," Lisa said. "Won't it be kind of hard to get rid of?"

"Yeah, but I'm going to start racing on my own soon, and this is what it takes."

"So racing runs in the family, huh?"

"I guess."

"Well, tell your mom I called. Nothing urgent."

/////

Jamie raced the next weekend, but there was something missing. She won easily, but not having Chad behind her to push her was a loss. She drove the track like a pro and nearly lapped the field, but she lost her concentration and almost forced the guy into the wall. He was a friend of Trace Flattery's.

"Sorry about that," she said to Trace after the race.

"What's up with you, Jamie?" Trace said. He winced as he ripped his headphones from his rather large ears. "You act like you're in some other world."

I want to be, she almost said. She apologized again and went back to the garage and the solitude of her car.

If she'd been told a year earlier—or even a few months ago—that she wouldn't have Chad breathing down her neck, she'd have been ecstatic. But that wasn't true anymore. All she could think of was his move up. She heard he was going to qualify for a race near Atlanta the following weekend. He was doing what she wanted to do.

Easter had come and gone. Her mom had bought her a new dress from Kohl's, and she felt like a little kid with a basket of candy. True, it seemed like a bribe to get her to go to church willingly, but it was a good one. She got stares from the guys in the back row as she walked by.

Trace had approached her in Sunday school and nervously said, "You look real pretty today."

She rolled her eyes. "And that's a change?"

"I just meant, you normally don't dress up like that and . . ."

"I know what you meant," she mumbled. She felt bad shooting him down, but what did he expect?

/////

Jamie drove the white auto-parts truck to the Devalon garage in nearby Mooresville for a delivery late one afternoon. The sun was staying up later as winter let go of its subtle grasp on the Charlotte area. People imagined tons of snow when they heard North Carolina, but the winters were generally mild. When spring hit, though, all of nature budded and sprung full force.

She stepped out of the truck with the package of parts and walked up the brick walkway lined with shrubs and finely manicured grass. It looked like a golf course. The Devalon garage was a rambling complex that seemed more like a car museum compared to her dad's garage. Huge bay doors lined either side of the structure, and at the front was an opulent office, complete with a case of trophies and a gigantic picture of the lead driver in his all-black leather outfit.

The girl at the front desk smiled and signed the delivery form. Her smile was sticky sweet, like a prom queen who hated her date. The woman probably felt like slapping a puppy, but it was her job to show her teeth and be pleasant. "Thank you," she said.

The familiar sound of air wrenches and the smell of hot oil filled Jamie's senses as she walked past the garage. She was checking her clipboard for her next delivery when someone came up behind her.

"Hello, Jamie."

"Oh, hello, Mr. Devalon. Thought you'd be getting ready for Phoenix."

He nodded. "Headed out tomorrow."

"Congrats on the All-Star Challenge. I'm sure you'll do well."

"It's not that big of a deal. Been there before and hope to be again. Your dad ever make it?"

She knew *he* knew that her dad never had. It was just another instance of him trying to put someone in their place. "I don't think so. And it doesn't look like he'll make it this year."

"He's had some tough luck. I'm sure he'll overcome all this adversity. Always seems to."

Jamie nodded and turned to the truck.

"Hold up there." Mr. Devalon walked to the truck and leaned against the door, covering the logo. "Our owner's coming to the track next week. Chad's been making progress, getting ready for his first race in the new division, and he wants to take a look at him and his times. How about you coming over and giving it a shot?"

"I would, but I don't have a car yet. I'm trying to sell my—"

"Use ours."

"Chad's?"

"Sure, why not?"

"How's he going to feel about it?"

He laughed. "You let me take care of that. He'll be fine. What was it you said about him pushing you to be your best? Now you can return the favor."

Jamie tucked the clipboard under an arm and kicked at the gravel in the driveway. "Why are you doing this, Mr. Devalon? Why are you being so nice to me?"

He pulled out a piece of nicotine gum, crossed his arms, and looked off toward the lake behind the garage. "I don't know. Maybe I'm trying to change my image. Maybe I want to be known as kind and gentle to the weaker sex."

Jamie rolled her eyes. *Maybe he's up to something. But what?*

Mr. Devalon uncrossed his arms and opened the truck door. "Or maybe I see talent and figure the only way it's gonna get noticed is if I give you a little help. Five o'clock next Tuesday."

SOMEBODY ONCE SAID that no man is an island, but Tim made himself one. He didn't know who had said that because he didn't pay much attention in English class. Tim went to school and did his homework (for the most part) and steered clear of anyone from the church.

Each day since he'd been fired from his job, he'd lingered around his locker until the buses left and the hallways cleared. From school, he walked to the nearby library and stayed in a room downstairs until dark, then walked home through a wooded area. To say he was skittish about being attacked by Jeff and his friends was an understatement. He even taped a piece of paper over the small window in the library study room so no one could see inside.

He found enough reading material

in the library, but he always returned to his father's diary. Through those pages he seemed to understand more and more about his dad.

In an entry that came a few months after his wife had left, Tim's dad wrote about a momentous change.

Something happened today that I can't really explain. I've never been religious. I've never gone to those chapel services and think it's mostly a show. But I've been at such a low point that I'm tempted to just turn to the bottle. Instead, today I picked up a little booklet one of the chaplains left with me when he heard what had happened. Said he'd be praying for me.

The booklet was called "When Someone You Love Is Gone," and it was about going through loss and how God is the only one we can lean on. I think it was probably written for people who face the death of a wife or husband, but it feels like Lexy has died now that she left Tim and me.

I read the whole thing from front to back and then started over again. I always thought

God was there but pretty much left him alone. This makes me think he cares about me and wants to help if I'll let him. I looked up the verses it listed, and it took a long time because I don't know much about the Bible. Couldn't find half of them. But the ones I did find sure make sense. I think I'm on my way to someplace. Where it takes me, I don't know, but I want to be a good dad to Tim and show him I can make something of myself.

Tim closed the book, unable to continue. He'd noticed a difference in his dad a few months after his mom had left, but that was so long ago he'd just gotten used to it. He was never pushy about going to church, because they were always on the road, but he did go to the chapel services. Had the whole religion thing worked for him?

The lights clicked off in the library, and Tim grabbed his stuff and made it out before the security guard noticed him. He stuffed the diary in his backpack and walked the lit sidewalk, swatting at no-see-ums and thinking about his dad. A car drove slowly beside him and stopped. His heart beat faster, and he looked for a place to run.

Finally he got the nerve to turn and saw a girl

talking on her cell phone. The thought of Jeff and his crew frightened him, but he was struck with another thought: if religion had worked for his dad, would it work for him?

No way. Couldn't.

Tim passed a shopping center and cut through the parking lot on his way toward the forest. Still deep in thought, he tried to piece together the fragments of his life. He had so many questions. If his dad's religion was so important to him, why hadn't he talked more about it? What had caused his mother to leave? Did she get tired of life on the road, meet some other guy, or not want to take care of him?

A car engine revved and rattled. Tires squealed, and then doors opened. Tim turned to see Jeff and the two goons almost on him. It took him only a second to assess the situation and take off. He didn't have great brains or brawn, but one thing he could do was run. He raced for a chain-link fence at the other side of the parking lot. With one motion, he threw the backpack over, jumped for the top, and caught it, then cartwheeled over the two strands of barbed wire.

He snagged his backpack as the three made it to the fence, laughing and gasping for air.

"What's so funny?" Tim said.

Jeff pointed to the pond behind Tim. "You know where you are?"

Tim looked around. He'd walked through here for the past few weeks and vaguely remembered a sign on the front of the building.

"It's the reptile park, numskull," one of Jeff's friends said.

Tim turned and stared at two eyes on the surface of the pond. A tail swished in the water at the edge of the pond and sent a chill through him.

Jeff moved back and jumped, scaling the fence.

Tim took off for the front of the park.

"Cut him off!" Jeff yelled, hitting the ground. "Oh, you're not gonna get away from us this time, loser!"

The front gate was locked and so was the building, but Tim found another fence small enough to scale and ran full force into it. He was almost over when something tugged at his backpack. It was Jeff, ripping it from his shoulder.

Tim wasn't about to lose his one connection with his dad, so he slipped back from the fence and landed with a thud.

Jeff unzipped the pack and dumped the contents on the ground, kicking and ripping Tim's composition book to pieces.

"Stop!" Tim lunged at Jeff, who deftly moved back.

"Stop! Auntie Em, stop!" the two mocked from the other side of the fence.

Tim held up a hand in front of Jeff. "This fight is between you and me. Tell them to stay on the other side of the fence."

Jeff picked up the diary and leafed through it. "What do we have here? Says Martin Carhardt in the front. This must be your old man's."

"Put it down."

The other two scaled the fence just as Jeff tossed the diary into the gator pond.

Tim ran to the edge and watched the diary float. As he took a step into the water, something green and menacing rose to the surface and splashed. The diary disappeared.

"I didn't know gators could read," Jeff said, and the other two laughed.

Seething, Tim turned on them and rushed in a fury. He swung and kept swinging, hoping he'd hit something, tears streaming, out of breath and patience. He'd read somewhere that the Bible said it was better to give than receive, and he wanted to give a lot more than he took. He'd also heard people who were hit were supposed to turn the other cheek.

Another reason religion wasn't for him.

TIM WALKED INTO A brick building surrounded by cars. A popular spot. The first floor had an office listing in a glass case. It smelled like alcohol, and people were sitting in plastic chairs in the hallway, waiting their turn for something. It gave Tim the creeps.

He stepped out of the elevator on the third floor. A sign at the end of the hall said it was the Department of Children and Family something or other. It was quieter up here, and Tim walked back and forth a few minutes, trying to get the nerve to go through the door. He turned around and even pushed the Down button on the elevator, but he finally walked into the office.

Inside he found more chairs. A section for kids with puzzles and wooden blocks and Tinkertoys. Lots of magazines everywhere.

"May I help you?" a woman said from behind the desk. It had a long top with a sign-in sheet.

"I'm looking for Lisa," he said.

"She's out right now on a case. Did you have an appointment?"

"No, ma'am."

"Well, let me call her and tell her you're here. What was the name?"

Tim told her and sat.

A few minutes later a young mom walked in with a curly-haired baby who couldn't stop crying. She carried the child on her hip, like she was some kind of baby pimple. When she put the kid on the floor, the baby screamed even more. Then she saw Tim and cried harder, clear snot running down. Tim tried to play peekaboo to get the little thing to settle down, but it was no use.

"She's teethin'," the mom said. "It ain't got nothin' to do with you."

From her voice, Tim could tell the mom was only a girl, probably not a lot older than him.

"Tim," the receptionist said, "I just talked with Lisa. She said to wait in her office. She'll be back in 15 or 20 minutes."

The woman showed him to a corner office with a window overlooking some trash bins. Lisa's desk was neat compared to the trailer, but there were several stacks of papers and forms. He wondered how many people she talked to each week.

Her computer was in screen-saver mode. It flashed pictures of her and a dark-haired guy—he guessed it was her husband. One was taken by the beach with a big heart drawn in the sand. Another looked like it was a concert, both of them holding up ticket stubs. More photos showed groups of people waving, a baby in a crib, an older woman in a wheelchair, and some girls in pajamas hanging on to a younger Lisa. All of them smiling.

Does anybody you know ever not *smile?* Tim thought.

When Lisa walked in, Tim was looking over the books in her bookshelf. She plopped her purse on the floor and closed the door. "See anything interesting?"

"Sorry. I was just looking."

"No, it's fine. I never read them anymore. If you see something you like, just take—" She drew closer and looked at his face. "Tim, what happened to you?"

He sat and folded his hands in his lap. "Had a run-in with a chain-link fence and a couple guys who wanted to introduce me to it."

"Did you have that looked at?"

"In a mirror, yeah."

She examined the bruises and scrapes. "Did Tyson do this? You're not protecting him, are you?"

He shook his head. "He's a real jerk, but he's never hit me."

She sat back in her chair and looked at him the same way one of his teachers at school did. Like he was a wet pup in the rain and they wanted to let him in but couldn't because he wouldn't come.

"How did you get here?" she finally said.

"Bus."

"You didn't have school today?"

"I did, but I figured this was more important."

"What can I do for you?"

"That family in North Carolina. You think the offer's still good?"

"I haven't talked with them for a couple of weeks, but the last time I did they said to tell you if you ever change your mind, they'd be glad to come get you." She folded her hands. "What about your dad? about what happened at Talladega?"

"The way I figure it, the guy probably feels guilty and wants to make himself feel better. They have a nice house?"

She pulled an envelope from her desk drawer and handed him a picture. Dale Maxwell stood on the porch of a blue house with his arm around a pretty, red-haired woman. In front of them was a younger kid with a missing tooth, smiling. Beside him was a girl, a few years older. He recognized her from the Daytona broadcast. She looked a lot like her mother but with an attitude. Arms crossed. Lips together. No smile. A few freckles on her cheeks.

"Nice house," Tim said.

"They're really good people. They want to help you."

"How soon do you think I should go up there?"

"I'll call and ask if they're still willing to pick you up. Would you be more comfortable taking a bus? Maybe fly?"

"Whatever they want. I'm ready to go as soon as you can get me there."

She called and left a message on the Maxwells' answering machine. "I'll call you as soon as I hear from them."

JAMIE'S MOM WENT INTO hyperdrive cleaning the house and getting the downstairs room cleared of boxes and buying a new mattress for the creaky old bed from their grandparents' house. Jamie vaguely remembered how her mom had gotten Kellen's room ready weeks before he was born. She called it nesting.

If Jamie were honest with her parents, she would have admitted that she hated the idea of someone interrupting their life. Things were hard enough the way it was, but for some guy to come live with them for who knew how long was just plain dumb. But with both of them set on the idea and Kellen looking forward to outnumbering the girls, she was the odd man out.

The offer from Devalon to race Chad's car ate at her all weekend. She worked on Saturday and on one run took the long way around so she could drive by the Devalon garage. Chad's car—at least the one she assumed was his—was outside, new decals on the side. It was already filled with sponsors, including a huge Devalon decal and the #13, like his dad.

She'd run through the conversation several times in her head, telling her dad about the Devalon car and taking a practice run. She knew what he'd say, though.

The only person who knew about it was Cassie Strower, and Jamie had sworn the girl to secrecy.

"You have to at least tell your dad," Cassie had said. "What if something happens?"

"Then my career gets cut short. At least I'll know I tried."

"No, what if something good happens and you get a chance to race for them? How's your dad going to feel knowing you kept this a secret from him?"

"You worry too much."

"You know I'm right," Cassie said. "Otherwise you wouldn't have told me."

"I told you because . . ."

"What?"

"Because I thought you'd understand. Obviously I was wrong."

Cassie put an arm on her shoulder. "I'm just saying I think you'd feel better if they knew about this. You told me your dad said he was *for* you, not against you, in your dream to race."

"Sometimes I think they say that stuff to soften me up for the letdown." She turned toward Cassie. "You know how it was when you were a little kid and it'd be snowing outside, and the only thing you could think of was getting out there and riding that sled as fast as you could or building a fort and having a snow-ball battle? But parents want you to stay warm and not go outside, or if they let you, you have to put so many layers of clothes on you can't move."

"I always liked wearing big coats and gloves."

Figures, Jamie thought. "Parents want to keep you cooped up. They want to block your dreams."

"Why would they do that?"

"I don't know. Maybe they're scared of what might happen. Scared I'll fail."

"Or get hurt."

"Cassie, have you ever felt like you were meant to do something? I mean, really made to accomplish something big?"

Her friend nodded. "I know exactly how it feels."

"You?"

Cassie looked away, then turned back. "I've never told anybody this, but one night I was reading this story about a missionary who went to this foreign country and had all kinds of trouble telling people about God and what he'd done. And I must have fallen asleep reading, but then I woke up and it was dark outside, and the lights were on in my room, and I just had this feeling that I was going to do the same thing. Not go to a foreign country necessarily but tell a lot of people about God."

"You heard a voice?"

"No, not an actual one, but it felt as clear as hearing you talk to me right now."

"That's weird."

"Yeah, I know. But in a strange way, I think I must feel the same as you do about racing."

Jamie sighed. "Your dream feels a lot more spiritual than mine."

"No way. Maybe God made you to go fast. Maybe he wants to use you on the track. I just think it's better to tell your parents about this Devalon thing before you get in too deep."

Jamie stared at the #13 car until her truck radio squawked. "Hey, Jamie, where are you?"

"I'm almost there," she said, shifting into first and spinning her tires.

TIM GOT OFF THE bus and walked through the neighborhood filled with old houses. He had gotten a phone number for Briarcliff Elementary and talked with someone in the office there. As it turned out, he was more than a mile from the right stop, but he kept walking.

He finally found the street and checked the information against the address he had written down. After several blocks he came to the single-story ranch house on a quiet street. He recognized the car in the driveway and got on his hands and knees and looked underneath. There was no leak, and the stain on the driveway looked dry.

He rang the doorbell, and a yippy dog barked in the window, standing on the back of the couch. The curtain moved at the side of the window. Then the door opened slightly, the chain on the back of the door still attached.

"Yes?" a woman said. "Can I help you?"

"Hi there. I don't know if you remember me. You gave me a ride not long ago."

"Tim!" Mrs. Rubiquoy closed the door and unlatched the chain. "Come on in. Brutus, calm down."

Brutus rushed over and sniffed Tim's shoes and the cuffs of his pants. The dog's eyes were bugged out, and his ears stood straight up.

"Doesn't look like a Brutus to me." Tim laughed. He sat, and the dog jumped up beside him and warily climbed onto the back of the couch. "I see your car's not leaking anymore."

"Yes, the garage said they didn't get the . . . what was it?"

"Freeze plug?"

"Yes, that's it. They got it all fixed, and I haven't had a problem again. Can I get you something to drink?"

"No, ma'am, I'm fine. Just came here to return something."

"Oh?" She sat on the edge of the couch at the other end. Brutus edged closer to her.

"You knew I took something from your purse the day you gave me a ride."

Her eyes darted around the room.

He pulled out the $100 bill. "I don't think you put this out for me to see for no reason. You thought I'd take it."

Mrs. Rubiquoy nodded, and a hint of a smile came to her face. "But the fact that you've brought it back proves something to me."

"What's that?"

"That I wasn't wrong about you. It was an experiment. If I never heard from you again, I'd just given a $100 contribution to a young man's life. But if your conscience got the best of you and I *did* hear back . . . well, you're proving I was right about you all along."

Tim shook his head. "I don't know how this proves anything but that I'm a low-down, dirty thief who takes money from old ladies. No offense."

She smiled and pointed to a picture on the mantel. "That's my husband. He had an uncanny ability to pick people for his work who turned into the most wonderful employees. His company gave him an award for it once. And when they asked how he weeded out the bad from the good, do you know what he said?"

"I can't say that I do."

"He said that most people are really good workers. They just don't have confidence." She placed a wrinkled hand on Brutus, and the dog closed his eyes. "I don't know how you got those scratches or how life has slapped you upside the head. I don't even know how our paths crossed that day. But I do know *why*. God wants you to know you're a good boy, Tim. He has something special for you. He wants to work through you."

"I'm not sure I even believe in God."

"Well, that's okay. He believes in you." She handed the $100 bill back to him. "Now you go out and take the world by the horns, and don't forget that there's an old lady down here in Florida waiting to hear that you've found the Lord. Okay?"

He stared at the money with a feeling of weight being lifted from his shoulders, as if the woman had just taken away a hundred pounds from him.

"Have you had anything to eat?" she said.

"Not yet. I thought I'd stop and get a burger on my way home."

"I know a good place around the corner. Then I'll drive you home."

"You don't have to do that, ma'am."

"Why? You think I'm scared you're going to take more?" She laughed, and it was contagious.

ON TUESDAY JAMIE SLIPPED out of the house decked out in her work uniform but headed to the track. When she got there, she changed into her fire suit and her orange helmet. She had her racing gloves and shoes as well, and when she walked to the railing overlooking the track, she almost turned around. Who was she kidding? Chad had a huge jump on her. She'd never even been around this track before.

The black #13 car roared past as several people watched from the pits.

She turned to leave but heard a voice calling from below. It was Mr. Devalon waving, pointing to the access road.

She hopped in her car and drove up to a security guard, who was on the phone. The man waved her through, and she parked by the garage and walked through a couple of gates toward the pits, her helmet under one arm.

Chapter 34

The scream of the engine sounded like music to her. She could see Chad in the far turn, accelerating out of it and speeding toward the finish line.

Butch Devalon was talking with a tall man—something about the race in Texas this coming weekend—when another man holding a stopwatch interrupted them.

"Look at this, sir," Stopwatch said. "We can confirm it with the chip, but that's not bad."

Butch Devalon waved Jamie over. "Jamie, I want you to meet the owner of the team. This is Mr. Hardwick."

She shook the older man's hand firmly. "Nice to meet you, sir."

"Call me Shane. I've heard a lot about you, Jamie. And I respect your dad's driving. What's he think of all this?"

"Uh, well, he's . . . open to me succeeding."

"That's a good way to put it," Mr. Devalon said. "We're looking forward to seeing what you can do."

Chad rolled into the pits, unhooked the window net, and climbed out. He was all smiles at his time, but that changed when he saw Jamie. "What are you doing here?" he said.

Jamie looked at Chad's dad, sensing the tension. "You didn't tell him?"

"Son, we're giving you a little competition here. Just to see what happens."

Chad grabbed the HANS device and shoved it into Jamie's gut. "Where's her car?"

"She's using ours."

"Mine?"

"No, *ours.* You didn't pay for it. Hop in there, Jamie. Let's see how fast you can go."

"Don't wreck it," Chad snarled.

Under any other circumstances she would have been excited. Chad's reaction had dampened her enthusiasm. As she clicked the six-point harness and snapped on her HANS device, she took a few deep breaths and tried to concentrate. Chad and his dad would have troubles with each other the rest of their lives. No reason she had to be in the middle. She was only taking a little ride around the track. No big deal. She popped the steering wheel on and locked it in place.

"Take it easy for the first two laps," Mr. Devalon said, leaning down and helping her get strapped in. "Get a feel for the car and the track. We'll wave the green flag for you. Take a cooldown lap after you get the checkered."

Jamie nodded and pushed in the clutch and put the car in first gear. The last thing she wanted to do was stall the thing in the pits, but that's what she did. The engine sputtered and died.

"That's okay," Mr. Devalon said. "It's a little sensi-tive today. Hit the switch again."

She went through the procedure, and the car fired to life. She imagined the voice over the loudspeakers saying, "Gentlemen and lady, start your engines!"

This time she was off, shifting into second, then third as she ran out of room on pit road and hit the middle of the first turn. It felt like she was going straight into the wall, but at the last second she turned left, punched it into fourth gear, and was gone.

"Woooooooooooooooo!" she yelled, slamming the pedal to the floor. She studied the track to find the racing groove that would give her the fastest lane around the track and backed off the accelerator as she hit the third turn. The engine whined as she dropped lower on the track. Then she hit the accel-erator again.

Speed. Pure speed. The engine was more powerful than anything she had ever driven. It felt so good— she wanted to scream!

As she passed the starting line, she glanced at Mr. Devalon and the others talking. Chad wasn't there.

The sun beat down, reflecting off the shiny sur-face of the car. The smells of oil and gas and the heat of the engine ran through the cockpit. The track had been cool during the day with cloud cover, which meant better speed for her and Chad, a firm grip for the tires but not too firm.

The accelerator was at the floor as she took the green flag. Jamie let up slightly in the turn but not much. She shot out to the backstretch and felt like she was flying. The wheel in her hands, the white lines of the track whizzing by, the blistering noise around her. For two laps she was in a zone, going as fast as she had ever gone, in complete control, with no one to tell her to back off, no one to tell her to take it easy.

When the checkered flag waved, she slowed a little, but it was too much fun not to take the first turn at full speed. She moved down to the apron after the third turn and rolled into the pit area.

"Looks like you've done that before," Mr. Devalon said as she climbed out and took off her helmet.

"What a blast!" Jamie smiled. She couldn't help it. It was the greatest feeling she'd ever experienced. "How was my time?"

"Ask the owner—he kept a clock on you."

The owner was talking on the phone when she got there. She'd blown it. She was sure of it.

"How'd it feel?" Mr. Hardwick said to her when he hung up.

"Incredible. That's a great car. Thanks for letting me drive it."

"You're not a bad driver, young lady," he said. "Your time was . . ."

"What?" Jamie said.

"I was just talking with the track manager. You came within .85 of a second of beating the qualifying record."

Her mouth dropped. "Really? I don't believe it." She felt like she would explode. All the years of racing anything with four wheels had paid off. She *could* go fast. And she wanted to go faster.

"Hold up," Chad said behind them. "I want another shot at her. What was the difference in our times?"

The owner showed him and Chad winced.

Mr. Devalon grinned. "Fair enough, Son. Go out there and show her."

Chad slammed on his helmet and got in the car, looking back at Jamie with a scowl. He spun the tires so they smoked as he raced onto the track.

Jamie moved to the wall and sat there, unable to hide her smile. *Almost beat the track record. A girl almost beat the track record!*

Now all the feelings about the guy from Florida coming to live with them and the other stuff that had her down melted. Her dream was coming into clearer focus. She didn't know how she'd get there, but she was going to get there. No matter what.

A squeal of tires brought her back, and she glanced to her right. Chad had driven full speed into the last turn and was losing it. Everyone turned as the #13 car shot up the incline and scraped the wall, then turned sideways and went airborne.

 **CHRIS FABRY** is a writer, broadcaster, and graduate of Richard Petty Driving Experience (top speed: 134.29 mph). He has written more than 50 books, including collaboration on the Left Behind: The Kids, Red Rock Mysteries, and the Wormling series.

You may have heard his voice on Focus on the Family, Moody Broadcasting, or Love Worth Finding. He has also written for *Adventures in Odyssey*, *Radio Theatre*, and *Kids Corner*.

Chris is a graduate of the W. Page Pitt School of Journalism at Marshall University in Huntington, West Virginia. He and his wife, Andrea, have nine children and live in Colorado.

RED ROCK MYSTERIES

BRYCE AND ASHLEY TIMBERLINE are normal 13-year-old twins, except for one thing—they discover action-packed mystery wherever they go. Wanting to get to the bottom of any mystery, these twins find themselves on a nonstop search for truth.

CP0140

The Wormling

Such was the fate of Owen Reeder, for as he took his last step of what could be called a normal life, something caught him at his waist. His feet and arms flew forward along with his head; then he snapped back. Owen was suspended in midair.

That's when he heard the whisper. . . .

"Courage, Owen."

From the minds of Jerry B. Jenkins and Chris Fabry comes a thrilling new action-packed fantasy that pits ultimate evil against ultimate good.

Available October 2007!

The Future Is Clear

Check out the exciting Left Behind: The Kids series